Point

my Funny Valentine

Karen McCombie

For Wendy, for all her help with my research
(ie an excuse for tea, biscuits and gossiping).

Scholastic Children's Books,
Euston House, 24 Eversholt Street
London NW1 1DB, UK
a division of Scholastic Ltd
London ~ New York ~ Toronto ~ Sydney ~ Auckland
Mexico City ~ New Delhi ~ Hong Kong

First published in the UK by Scholastic Ltd, 2002
This edition published by Scholastic Ltd, 2006

10 digit ISBN 0 439 96087 8
13 digit ISBN 978 0439 96087 8

Printed and bound by Nørhaven Paperback A/S, Denmark

10 9 8 7 6 5 4 3 2

Papers used by Scholastic Children's Books
are made from wood grown in sustainable forests.

my Funny Valentine

Omigod . . . under the lamppost nearest Jude's house. . .

[My stomach's just lurched in the weirdest way.]

It's a boy . . . maybe about seventeen . . . he's stopped . . . he's gazing up at the sky. . .

[*What's he looking at?* I wonder, raising my eyes to the clear, velvety sky and its sprinkling of stars. Nice . . . but not as interesting as this boy, who I'm staring at again now.]

His face is bathed in light from the lamp. . .

[My heart's beating so fast I'm getting *breathless*.]

He is. . .

[I never believed in lust at first sight before.]

He is absolutely *beautiful*. . .

Other books by Karen McCombie

The *Ally's World* series
A Guided Tour of Ally's World
My V. Groovy Ally's World Journal
The *Stella Etc.* series
Marshmallow Magic and the Wild Rose Rouge

To find out more about Karen McCombie,
visit her website
www.karenmccombie.com

contents

chapter one

Love at first drool

Date:	*Thursday 14th February*
State of mind:	*Deeply uninspired*
State of life:	*Dismal — apart from a case of long-distance lust...*

"Aaaaaaaaaaaaaaaaaaiiiiiiiiiiiiiiiiiiiiiiiiiiieeeeeeeeeeeeeeeee!"

That, if you want to know, is my mother. Don't worry – she is not being murdered.

"Eeeeeeeeeeeeeiiiiiiiiiiiiiiiiiiiiiiiiiaaaaaaaaaaaaaaaa!"

And that is my big sister Ruth. She's twenty. She is *also* not being murdered.

They are the only two people in the room screaming. My dad isn't screaming, but he is making this odd, surprised-sounding *"Harrumph!"* noise and is self-consciously trying to hug Boring Brian (my sister's boyfriend). Only Dad chickens out halfway into the hug, and turns it into a few manly pats on the back instead.

Boring Brian is blushing and smiling and trying not to crumple under my dad's over-enthusiastic patting.

Ah, but I've got something wrong here – Boring Brian is *not* Ruth's boyfriend. As of now, he is officially her *fiancé*. This is what they've just announced, and this is what all the screaming and back-thumping is about.

"Isn't that lovely, Shaunna? Your sister's *engaged*!"

Mum turns a little too quickly and catches me looking blank-faced. (Lucky she didn't catch me half-a-second earlier when I was wincing from the pain of her and Ruth's high-pitched howling.)

In a panic, I stick on a smile and nod back, hoping I'm coming across enthusiastic enough.

"Mmm!" I manage to mumble non-committally.

It's not that I'm cynical or hard-hearted or anything – *honestly* I'm not. I'm really pleased for Ruth, if that's what she wants. It's just that it's all so . . . *predictable*.

"Oh, Ruth, on Valentine's Day too!" Mum gushes at my sister, letting me relax my fake smile slightly. "It's *such* a surprise! And *so* romantic!"

Now there's my point – that last bit of what my mum's said? It's *so* not true. It is *so* not a surprise that Ruth and Boring Brian are engaged. I mean, they've been going out together since . . . well, practically since the dawn of time, and they've always made it totally clear that their life plan was to get engaged/married/have 2.4 children/an estate car and a Tesco Club Card, and anything else would be a big let-down. I'd have been more surprised if they'd announced that they weren't *ever* going to get engaged, or that they were splitting up. But this? This is about as surprising as the Ten o'clock News having depressing bits

2

in it, or being told that cats go miaow and dogs go woof.

And as for romantic? They got engaged on *Valentine's* Day. I'm sorry, but that's not romantic – that's just *corny*.

"Oh, Mum, it was so fantastic!" Ruth is saying, clutching Mum's hands. "Brian took me to Franco's tonight –"

Now you see; that proves my point again. Franco's is this glorified takeaway pizza place that's been running ads all week in the local paper saying, *"Hey fellas – why not treat that special lady to a two-for-the-price-of-one pizza deal for Valentine's Day?"* Why not? I'll tell you why not – because it's naff, *that's* why not. Specially when the ad goes on to promise *"a candle on every table!"*, like that's some big wow. It's just that if Boring Brian *had* to propose on Valentine's Day (pass me the sick-bucket, please), why couldn't he do something like . . . I dunno, like . . . ask Ruth to marry him down at the beach at midnight, under the moon and stars, with the dark sea crashing spectacularly in the background. . . Not in sodding two-for-the-price-of-one Franco's, along with every other sucker who thinks a candle rammed in a bottle and some cheesy taped Italian music playing in the background is the height of romance.

"– and then this man came round the tables selling flowers," Ruth is gushing, "and Brian bought me a single red rose –"

Arrgghhhh! Not a single red rose, Brian! You could have surprised her with a bunch of beautiful tulips; an armful of arum lilies; a fistful of freesias; a bundle of buttercups. . . Ten-out-of-ten for choosing the *least* original flower in the world!

"– and then Brian went down on one knee and said to me, 'Ruth –'"

Oh, no – Mum's got her hand to her mouth, like she can't believe what's coming next.

"– he said, 'Ruth . . . will you marry me?'!"

Why is Mum gasping? Brian wasn't exactly going to get down on his knees and say, "Ruth – I'm a transvestite, and I'm leaving tomorrow to work on a cruise liner as a Jane McDonald tribute act!" (Although it would have been a lot more interesting if he had. . .)

Now Mum and Ruth are hugging, and – I'm pretty sure – crying, while Dad and Brian beam at them and each other and silently nod a lot. Me? I'm not sure what to do. I know I should be joining in the girlie hug-fest, but I'd feel like a big, fat fake. So, I just stand, like one of the boys, beaming and nodding.

"And you know the best thing, Mum?" Ruth sniffles happily, and shoots a watery-eyed look at her proud fiancé.

"What's that, sweetie?" asks Mum, ferreting out a paper tissue from somewhere up her sleeve and dabbing at her eyes.

"We've decided to get married. . ."

My sister pauses for dramatic effect, but my heart's already sinking, 'cause I just *know* what she's going to say.

". . .*next* Valentine's Day!" Ruth squeals.

"*Aaaaaaaaaaaaaaaaiiiiiiiiiiiiiiiiiiiiiieeeeeeeeeeeeeeeeeee!*"

Urgh – Mum's off again.

"I know! *Eeeeeeeeeiiiiiiiiiiiiiiiiiiiiiaaaaaaaaaaaa-aaaaaa!*"

And they're both back doing the hugging and crying

thing, and if I don't escape in two seconds flat I won't have any eardrums left.

"Listen! I'm going to nip across to Jude's and tell her the news!" I say, coming out with the perfect response to get me out of there and still look like I'm impressed by the whole not-very-surprising surprise announcement.

"OK, love," Mum nods distractedly in my direction, too excited to look at her watch and comment that it's nearly ten o'clock and a bit late on a school night to go disturbing the Conrads.

Ruth gives me the sweetest, wibbly-wobbly little smile and wiggles her fingers at me. She's lovely, my sister, even if she does settle for ordinary.

"And remember, Shaunna!" Ruth blinks at me, all dewy-eyed. "There's only *one* person I want as my bridesmaid!"

I'm kind of hoping she's talking about Justine or Penny or one of her other mates when she says that, but I have this funny feeling (called dread) that it's *me* she wants to see in a flouncy frock. . .

As it happens, Mum is wrong: "the Conrads" are only too glad to be disturbed. At least the one who's at home is. Jude flings open the door to me and says, "Thank God! A human!" and ushers me in.

See, my mum doesn't *get* that other people don't live exactly the same as us. You know; two, smiley parents who stay home in the evenings watching *Casualty* and *The Weakest Link*, two nice daughters who work hard (me at school doing GSCEs; Ruth at college studying Hotel Management), in our nice, cosy house. Jude's set-up is slightly different – maybe she lives in a practically identical house across the street, but, in *her* living room, there's no mum tut-tutting at Anne Robinson's rudeness. After being dumped by Jude's dad a few years back, her mum spent six months in a pit of gloom, then rose phoenix-like to take on the world – which involved ditching the "Mrs" tag and getting everyone (including Jude) to call her by her first name (Helen); studying for a degree; getting a whole new bunch of (much younger) friends from university; and basically managing somehow – in the midst of all the hard studying and hard partying – to forget the fact that she's got a fifteen-year-old daughter she's meant to be looking after.

"Where's Helen tonight?" I ask, following Jude through the hall.

"Who knows?" shrugs Jude, reaching for a big cardie that's draped over the end of the banister. "She's on this planning committee for some rally or something about student loans. They're supposed to be organizing it tonight, which probably means they're all in a *pub* somewhere."

Ooh, that came out a bit bitter. That's the trouble; *I* think Jude's mum is pretty inspirational (Helen's been planning a rally this evening while *my* mum's been planning tomorrow night's *tea*), but I know it's tough on Jude. It's hard to get your head around the fact that your mum is having a better social life than you.

"Um, where are we going?" I ask, as Jude hauls on the duvet-sized cardie and heads for the back door.

"Got to have a smoke," she replies, waving a cigarette at me. "I'm having a crisis."

Me and Molly hate the fact that Jude smokes. So does

her mum, which is why we are now going to perch ourselves on the bench at the bottom of the garden in the freezing cold, so that no tell-tale fumes can slither anywhere near the house, and give her away. Luckily, Jude only ever smokes when she's having a crisis. Unluckily, she tends to have about thirty crises a week.

"What's up?" I frown, pulling the sleeves of my jumper down over my hands as I stomp after her down the path.

"Got that thingy test tomorrow and I haven't studied for it," she says, flopping on to the flaky wooden bench that faces away from the garden and house and into the dark leafiness of Westburn Park, just beyond the high, metal-railed fence.

"Why haven't you studied for it?" I ask Jude, sitting myself next to her and hugging my knees up to my chin.

"Dunno. I tried to . . . but I got distracted, and then . . . just didn't get round to it."

Loads of people would love to live in a house free of nagging parents – like me, even if mine are the kind that try and *coax* you along rather than the kind who threaten to kneecap you if you don't tidy your knicker drawer or whatever. But Jude, she's the sort of girl that *needs* someone nagging her – nicely or not – or she never gets anything done. And Helen's got this optimistic view that Jude's grown-up enough and responsible enough to sort her own life out. Ha – fat chance.

"Anyway, distract me," Jude pleads. "I don't want to think about tests and . . . and. . ."

She's wafting her horrible, smelly cigarette in the air while she thinks what she's trying to say.

"*Not* having swotted for tests?" I suggest helpfully.

7

"Yeah, *that*," she grumbles bleakly. "So, go on – what's brought you skipping over here?"

And so I tell her about Ruth and Boring Brian, and their cheesy engagement in cheesy old Franco's. And Jude goes all melty on me.

"Don't you see what I mean, though?" I say, slightly exasperated and flapping her smoke away. "It's just that I *know* it's nice for Ruth and everything, but don't you think it's just all too corny?"

"Shaunna, it's *never* going to happen like *you* want it," Jude grins at me, which exasperates me even more. "You think love's all about some *special* boy coming along and *whisking* you off to New Mexico on the back of his motorbike, where you'll sit beside a campfire in the desert, listening to him strumming his guitar and playing a song he's written *specially* for you, and every morning you'll wake up with a cactus rose placed on your pillow that he's plucked for you at dawn. . ."

"OK! OK! Quit it!" I stop her, hating hearing her trash one of my favourite fantasies.

What gets me is that all the girls I know – including Jude and Molly – they go out with these lads who seem to communicate in the language of Grunt. They think "special" is if a boy phones when he says he will. I don't want to sound pushy here, but there've got to be boys out there with more soul, more imagination than that. Haven't there? So, yeah, I *do* day-dream about being whisked off into the heat and dust of New Mexico by someone amazing. I *do* yearn for a boy who'd want to write a song for me, or paint my portrait, or name a star after me. But it's not like I live on Planet Airhead and think that stuff is the only way someone can prove they're special. I'd settle for a lad that would send me a card, just saying something stupid like, "Hi, Shaunna – happy Thursday!" Or a boy who'd drape daisy chains around my neck. Or a guy who wanted to make snow angels in the park in the middle of winter. . .

"You've got to get real, Shaunna," Jude gently nags at me in a school-teacher tone, "or you'll *never* get a boyfriend."

Now that really, *really* bugs me. OK, so I'm fifteen and have never had a boyfriend. And while that hacks me off sometimes, at least I'm not like Jude, who's been out with loads of losers and had her heart broken by every single, last, loser one of them. If she can't even see the irony in that, then I'm not going to try and explain it to her. In fact, I'm so mad, I can't even answer her, so I just stare off into the park – where I can hear the distant cackle of laughter – and ignore her.

In the daytime, the park is really pretty, in a standard trees/flowers/fountain/bandstand kind of way. But I kind of like it more now, all dark and Gothic, with its few curlicued Victorian streetlamps dotted around the paths, casting a weird mustardy glow over everything. All the neighbours whose houses back on to the park – like Jude's – they're always writing into the local paper to moan about the gangs of juvenile thugs/ assorted weirdos/potential burglars they're convinced sneak in there and loiter with intent once the park is locked up.

Me and Jude think they're just a right a load of spoilsports – the old fogey neighbours, I mean. It's only ever kids mucking about, and that's only 'cause there's not much to do round here at nights, specially in winter. In fact, I can hear more of the distant laughter now – and it just sounds like a bunch of lads, not rampaging hooligans or anything. It's not like there's every any real troub—

Omigod . . . under the lamppost nearest Jude's house. . .

[My stomach's just lurched in the weirdest way.]

It's a boy . . . maybe about seventeen . . . he's stopped . . . he's gazing up at the sky. . .

[*What's he looking at?* I wonder, raising my eyes to the clear, velvety sky and its sprinkling of stars. Nice . . . but not as interesting as this boy, who I'm staring at again now.]

His face is bathed in light from the lamp. . .

[Yikes – my heart rate has surged from 0 to 150 in five seconds. What's going on?]

His dark hair is flopping back to show off sharp cheekbones . . . sort of Slavic eyes. . . He is. . .

[My heart's beating so fast I'm getting *breathless*.]

He is. . .

[I never believed in lust at first sight before.]

He is . . . absolutely *beautiful*. . .

"I know *I'd* love it if someone wanted to buy *me* a red rose," Jude suddenly starts mumbling, "never mind ask me to *marry* them."

[The spell the boy's cast over me is broken, and instantly my heart rate calms down slightly – mainly because I've remembered to take a breath again, after unconsciously holding it for the last 60 seconds.]

"Shhh!" I hiss at Jude, grabbing her by the arm and

pointing over to the boy standing under the lamp.

He's still there, alone, blinking up at the stars and the moon. . .

"Looks a bit dodgy to me," Jude frowns, leaning forward and screwing up her eyes for a better look.

"He's not dodgy – he's *gorgeous*!" I whisper, watching him move away from the pool of light under the lamp and head for the silhouetted bandstand.

"If he's not dodgy, then what's he doing hanging around on his own like that for?" Jude whispers back.

"I don't know! Let's just watch him!" I tell her in my teeny-tiniest voice.

As my eyes adjust to the darkness, I can make out his shape – long and lean – sitting down on the steps of the bandstand, where he reaches down and pulls out . . . I don't know what, exactly.

"What the hell is *that*!" squeaks Jude.

"It's . . . it's. . ." I say frantically, straining my eyes and hoping this vision of beautiful boy-ness isn't going to turn out to be a park pervert after all.

"Whatever it is, it's huge!" Jude sniggers.

"Look! Look! He's lifting it up! It's OK! It's a telescope!" I cry out in relief, then slap my hand over my mouth, hoping he hasn't heard me. He hasn't (phew).

Yes! He's still a vision of beautiful boy-ness, and he's a beautiful boy who is right at this moment lost in the rings of Saturn, or the swirling red dust of Mars, or the deep, unfathomable recesses of the moon. . .

As I gaze at him star-gazing, I realize I'm holding my breath again, and Jude might be too, she's gone so quiet.

Oops – he's heard something. . . He's suddenly

dropped the telescope from his eyes and is casting around sharply – stopping (gasp!) and staring for a second in our direction. Can he really see us? Aren't we lost in the darkness, tucked away from the house lights behind us and the streetlamps in front of us? Or has the pinprick of orange light from Jude's cigarette signalled to him that he's being spied on? Part of me desperately wants our drool-fest to stay secret, but part of me is frantically sending out magnetic beams from my eyes to his. . .

But in two seconds flat, it's all over; as quickly as he appeared, the boy is gone – swallowed up by a baying bunch of boys who have just swooped and thundered along the path, shouting at him that the park-keeper's coming.

"Huh! Here we go!" Jude grumbles, turning around and noticing lights flickering into life in nearby houses. "Nosy neighbours, to your windows, double-quick time, please!"

But I don't look round – I'm still trying to follow him; trying to work out which of the vanishing distant shadows is The Boy.

"Come on; let's go in – before one of the old farts spots me with a fag and reports me to Helen. . ." Jude jokes, standing up and shivering.

"Sure," I reply, following her back up the path.

But just before I step though the back door into the brightness and warmth, I take one quick, last look into the now-silent, inky dark-green of Westburn Park.

I only saw him for a couple of minutes and I might never see him again. But somehow I feel, in the pit of my madly fluttering stomach, that I won't be forgetting that boy – that Star-Boy – in a hurry. . .

chapter two

375 wedding dresses and counting...

Date: Saturday 23rd February

State of mind: Borrrreddddddd...

Sightings of Star-Boy: Less than zero

I tell you, walking into our house is like walking into a branch of WHSmith at the moment. Well, at least the wedding section of WHSmith. And there's still a year (minus one week) to go till the Big Day. We're going to look like the council's paper-recycling department by then...

"Have you found anything interesting, Shaunna?" Mum beams at me, as she puts down a cup of tea on the table next to me.

"Nope," I say, flicking through the pages of *Wedding and Frilly Frocks*, or whatever the title of the particular magazine Mum and Ruth have assigned me is (in my role as – argh! – Ruth's bridesmaid).

This Saturday afternoon, the Sullivan family (Women's Division only) are gathered around the dining table, scrutinizing and evaluating every wedding detail in print. Spread along the middle of the table are several coloured folders, in various degrees of bulge. Each folder has a sticker on, which reads "Dresses", "Wedding Stationery", "Flower Arrangements" or something equally bridal-ly, and our job is to search for and find items of possible interest, then tear them out and add them to Ruth's relevant Ideas Folder. (*Only* once your selection has been inspected and approved by Ruth, of course.)

"What – you haven't got anything yet?" Mum asks me, settling herself back down and picking up her scissors purposefully.

What I *have* got is snow-blindness, after looking at the acres and acres of white dresses in this mag. Honestly, you've never *seen* so many dresses. I started counting them; every last one, whether it was in a fashion feature or an ad, and got to 375 before I lost track, and then it seemed too boring to start again (when it was pretty boring the first time round).

"Oh, Mum! Don't you think Brian would look handsome in this?!" Ruth gasps, pointing at a grinning male model in a grey top hat and tails.

Honestly, it looks like something a *duke* would wear; either that or a doorman at a posh hotel. Whichever, it definitely doesn't work for a sales assistant from an electrical discount store on the industrial estate (no offence to Brian, who I'm sure would feel like a right pillock in that get-up anyway).

Ruth obviously doesn't agree (not that I'd say that sort of thing aloud) – as we speak, she's snip-snipping out the hotel doorman suit for the "Bridegroom" folder. Uh-oh – I'm starting to feel sorry for poor Boring Brian.

So far, I've contributed precisely zilch to the Ideas Folders (and I'm struggling hard to ignore the one marked "Bridesmaids' Dresses"). But I feel I owe it to Ruth to seem slightly enthusiastic, and now I might finally be on to something . . . it's an article on people who've made their weddings more unique and individual (Hurrah! There are some sane people out there!), and here on the sheeny-shiny pages of *Wedding and Frilly Frocks* is one bride, showing off a teetering pile of the sweetest, tiniest fairy cakes, all decorated with wobbly, pink icing lovehearts.

"Look!" I say, holding up the magazine to Mum and Ruth. "Look what this girl had instead of a wedding cake!"

Mum and Ruth squint at the photo, then give each other a knowing glance.

"I don't *think* so, Shaunna!" Mum laughs, as if I've just suggested that Brian and Ruth have a giant bacon *sarnie* instead of a cake.

"Weddings are all about *tradition*," Ruth smiles at me, patronizing me ever-so-slightly, even though I know she doesn't mean to. "I want to do this just right!"

By "just right", I know that my sister really means "just like everyone else's". So she *won't* be like Molly's hippy cousin Martha, who got married in a green velvet, Medieval Baebe-style dress in a candlelit castle, and she *won't* do what Jacqui Duncan's skint-but-happy brother did and have a huge, champagne-popping picnic with family and friends in Westburn Park after him and his girlie got hitched in the local registry office. Nope; my sister will do it by the book, and look pretty (because she is) and Brian will be proud (because anything Ruth wants is fine by him, he loves her so much), but there won't be anything about that day that will give the merest hint – even in the smallest detail – of their personalities. It'll be just another conveyor belt, frilly frocks wedding, and it'll stick in people's memories for about as long as candyfloss stays in your mouth.

OK, I know what you're probably thinking; that I've got some big downer on my sister, but I haven't. Ruth is that rare thing – a big sister who doesn't boss you about; who offers to lend you her hairdryer/make-up/Lil-lets without you asking (and doesn't flip out at you for helping yourself); and never *ever* takes the mickey out of your taste in boys, music or clothes. And God knows, our taste in all those three areas is pretty different (like, different *planets* different).

I guess the thing is that I'm disappointed for Ruth; disappointed that she doesn't want to do anything special or unique for her big day, I mean. But then I'm not surprised. I come from an ordinary family; a *very* ordinary family, and that's the trouble. My mum and dad are – like Ruth – totally nice, but they'd never dream of doing anything unpredictable. God, no.

It's like when it came to choosing our names; Ruth is Ruth after my dad's sister, who repaid the honour of having her niece named after her by emigrating to Australia and quickly losing touch with anyone she was even vaguely related to. Me? It might sound like my parents were visited by the inspiration fairy when it came to deciding what to put on my birth certificate, but that's about as far from the truth as you can get. If you know that my dad's name is Sean and my mum's is Sheena . . . well, go figure.

Playing safe is like an art for my parents. My mum thinks doing the Lottery is *wildly* decadent. Since I was seven years old, they've dragged me and Ruth (and Boring Brian too for the last couple of summers) to the same resort we've always gone to in Majorca, and look at me with confusion whenever I've suggested that maybe, just *maybe,* we could go to Greece or Cyprus or somewhere different for a change. They think Chinese food is as exotically weird as cannibalism; that belly-button piercings are a sign of juvenile dementia (which is why I haven't shown them mine yet); and can't understand what attraction young people can see in crowded, sweaty clubs when you could just be at home with a nice cup of tea and the radio on, if you want to tap your toes along to something.

Speaking of Chinese food, maybe *that's* what I am to my family . . . I'm dim sum to their steak and kidney pie. I'm a pierced belly button (which still nips a bit, actually) to their sensible gold studs. I'm a beach party in Goa, to their dinner and dance at a hotel in Marbella. . .

(OK, I know I'm going off on a strange tangent in my head here, but it sure beats looking at pages and pages of forks and knives for "that perfect place setting". Oh, for one of those knives so I can end this torture now. . .)

"Shaunna! Shaunna!" Mum's voice cuts through my day-dreams. "Can you get the door, sweetheart?"

17

At last – an excuse to escape from the table for a minute, without looking like a moody, disinterested teenager. And it gets better – it's Molly and Jude. Even if they have no intention of staying, there's no way I can allow them to leave (I'll bribe them if I have to). They're my friends; it's their duty to rescue me from the misery that is the World of Weddings. . .

Course, I didn't have to bribe them. Well, as long as you don't count the tray of coffee and chocolate doughnuts that's plonked down on my bedroom carpet between the three of us.

"I hope you realize they're not going to let you wear *those* under your bridesmaid's dress!" Molly teases me, kicking the tip of my favourite grey felt Birkenstocks with the toe of her black zip-up ankle boots.

"And you know they're going to make you get a sensible haircut, don't you?" Jude grins.

I roll up on to my knees and stare at my reflection in the full-length wardrobe mirror. In a show of solidarity, Jude and Molly kneel on either side of me and stare into the mirror too.

"You don't think they'll want to do anything drastic, do you?" I ask, ruffling at my permanently ruffled long-ish, brown-ish hair. (When I got these choppy lays cut in, the stylist at the hairdresser assured me the look was called "tousled". Well, maybe it was shiny and "tousled" when he did it, but the best I can manage with my battered old hairdryer is "ruffled" and "messy" – but what the hell, I kind of like it this way.)

"Anything drastic? Well, there are bound to be curls. . ."

Molly tells my reflection, her face all mock-serious.

Her own almost-white blonde hair is pulled into stubby little plaits on either side of her reflection.

"Curls?!" I squeak.

"Heated rollers – that's what they'll do to you," Jude nods, probably very glad that her dark hair is cropped way too short to wrap a pair of tongs around.

"And there's bound to be a circlet of rosebuds. . ." Molly continues.

". . .or a tiara!" Jude concludes.

This is awful – I've been in denial all week, never really allowing myself to think what Ruth and Mum are going to force me into. . . And you know what? I'm not going to let it start now.

"So!" I say brightly, flipping away from the mirror and sprawling myself back across the carpet. "Any regrets about last night, girls?"

They've been teasing me, now it's my turn to tease them. Last night we went to a party at Scott Mason's house, which was surprising on a couple of counts. First, it's pretty surprising that we got invited at all, considering me and my two buddies aren't exactly part of Scott Mason's crew at school. He's one of those boys who is most definitely good-looking (in a sporty way), but hideously shallow (like those big showy Easter Eggs that have nothing inside them when you crack open the chocolate shell). He likes to surround himself with the kind of girls that we aren't; the pretty, perfect ones, preferably with big boobs and not much to say. To be honest, the only reason I think he invited us was to make up numbers – the more people at his party, the more popular he looked. And even if we didn't think much of Scott Mason, who were we to turn down an invitation to a perfectly good party?

Course, being there wasn't the only surprise.

"Regrets? No way!" grins Jude, looking just a tiny bit sheepish as she turns to face me and self-consciously hugs her knees right under her chin. "He's really cute!"

"Since when have you ever thought Scott Mason was cute? You always thought he was a big-headed boy bimbo!" I remind her, as I re-run the events of the previous evening in my head (ie, me saying "excuse me" five thousand times to the couple snogging on the stairs and blocking the way – then realizing it was Scott and *Jude*).

"I never really knew him before!" Jude shrugs.

"But snogging him doesn't change the fact that he's always come across like an arrogant git who only dates girls with long legs, short skirts and no brain!"

"Well, Scott still chose me, and I'm *none* of those things," Jude tells me defensively. "Maybe he's changed!"

"What – changed like he's had a personality transplant, you mean?" I smirk at Jude, who just shrugs back at me.

What definitely *hasn't* changed is Jude's big-time bad habit when it comes to boys, which works like this: she gets chatted up by some lad that she a) has nothing in common with, or b) has never remotely been attracted to, and is so flattered that she ends up snogging him. *Then* she spends the next few days/weeks trying to convince herself that she *does* fancy him, until everything goes horribly, miserably wrong – which is where me and Molly come in to pick up the pieces and say "there, there" (but never "I told you so").

Only I might be doing a double shift this time. . .

"And Nathan *Blake*?!" I squawk at Molly, who is presently studying her split ends and hoping I'm not going to bring up the fact that she was doing a superglued version of the salsa last night with Scott's best mate – the holder of the worst reputation in our school.

"He seems sweet!" Molly blinks at me.

Sweet? Nathan is as sweet as a bird-eating spider. He's trouble, with a capital *everything*.

"But, Mol – you *know* there were all those rumours about what went on with him and Shelly Benson!" I remind Molly, even though no one really knows what exactly *did* go on, only it probably didn't just involve holding hands.

"You know *your* trouble, Shaunna – you never give anyone a chance!" Molly comes back at me.

I know what she's trying to say – if I'd been up for it, last night there would have been three romantic encounters (and I use the term loosely). Ben Shapiro in our year has been making it obvious for months that he likes me, and – bless him – he made a super-human effort last night to flirt with me.

"Look, I don't fancy Ben – OK?" I dive in. "He's nice enough, but I don't fancy him!"

"But he really likes *you*! Why don't you just go out with him, just for a bit of fun?" Jude asks me, as serious as I am stunned.

"Jude, I could *never* go out with someone I didn't have feelings for!" I argue. "When I date someone, they have to really mean something to me. Y'know – be really special. Like . . . like. . ."

"Yeah, yeah – like that boy in the park last week," Molly drones flatly, crossing her arms and rolling her eyes.

"Well, yes!" I nod, ignoring her sarkiness. "He *was* special! How many boys do you know who stare at the stars?"

"Sounds like a bit of a dweeb to me!" Molly giggles, getting me back for giving her a hard time over Nathan, I suppose.

"No, actually, to be fair," Jude chips in, "I saw him too and he *was* pretty cute."

"But so what if he is?" says Molly. "He's just a piece of passing eye candy, Shaunna. There's no point in lusting after someone you might never see again and ignoring potential nice blokes 'cause you've got the hots for Space-Boy."

"Star-Boy," I mutter, correcting her.

(I know as a nickname it's pretty lame, but I've got to think of him as something, and no matter what Molly says, I'm definitely not going to ditch the vision I have of him seared in my mind in favour of any of the beer-guzzling, lechy losers at the party last night.)

"Well, if you want to be single for ever. . ." Molly tuts at me like a primary school headmistress.

"Hey!" Jude suddenly jumps in. "Shaunna might *not* be single for ever! You never know – in a year's time, she could be totally in love!"

"How do you figure that one out?" I ask her warily, wondering what's coming next.

"The wedding, of course!" Jude grins wickedly. "There's always supposed to be a bit of a thing between the bridesmaid and Best Man, isn't there?"

"Yeah!" Molly joins in. "So what gorgeous hunk is going to be Brian's Best Man, then, Shaunna!"

"Listen," I laugh back at both my friends, "I have no idea, but let's face it, if he's a friend of Boring Brian's then I'm never going to fancy him in a *million* years. But then I'm fussy – not like you two. . ."

For that, I get a dollop of cream splatted on my nose, and I guess I pretty much deserve it. . .

chapter three

One big happy family *(yeah like right!)*

Date:	Sunday 17th March
State of mind:	Frazzled
Sightings of Star-Boy:	Only in my dreams (worse luck)

I'm hunkered down on the cool grass, hidden out of sight behind the deeply scented rose bushes. (Note: the roses are a dark, bruised-purple colour. Not, I repeat, *not* red.)

He's there: staring at the stars again, lost in galaxies and meteor showers; maybe even tracking the lonely path of the international space station as it hurtles above the atmosphere, gazing back down on the planet and us and onward into infinity. . .

Should I speak? Or at least let myself be seen? If I stand up and pad softly across the springy park lawn, will he be startled to see someone come towards him in the dark, disturbing his reverie? Or will he instinctively know that

I'm a soul-mate, and motion for me to sit beside him, where his lean arms will encircle me as he holds his telescope up to my eye and lets me gaze into the night, at the fairy-lit heavens . . . and then—

"Adam!"

Bang goes my day-dream, and here I come slap-bang down to earth. Or at least the part of earth that belongs to 138, Tavistock Road, which in turn belongs to Mr and Mrs Pindar ("Call us Mary and Dave!") who just happen to be Boring Brian's boring parents.

"Adam, please don't do that! You know Bethany will just try to copy you!" Mrs Pindar (sorry – I can't bring myself to call her Mary) yelps at her youngest son (Brian's brother), who reluctantly removes the pea he's put up one nostril.

Across the table, Boring Brian's giggling two-year-old niece does indeed have to be restrained – by her heavily-pregnant mother – from copying her fifteen-year-old (going on seven-year-old) Uncle Adam and ramming a matching pea up her own nose.

Oh, this is going to be a long day. . .

We're here – me, Ruth, Mum and Dad ("Call us Sean and Sheena!") – for a getting-to-know-the-future-in-laws Sunday lunch. The thing is, we already *kind* of know the Pindars, or at least we used to; up until I was nine, they lived at the far end of our road. Far enough away so that Adam (he of the deeply unfunny pea gag) wasn't in my little neighbourhood gang, but close enough so that my older sister (who was allowed to stray further) got to hang out with her friend Boring Brian, who later turned into her boyfriend, although he never turned out any more interesting, as far as I could see.

Back when we were kids, Boring Brian would sometimes end up dragging Adam round to ours, and of those occasions I have vague – and not very pleasant – memories of being stuck with Adam, who'd pass the time by losing important bits of jigsaws, eating my crayons and trashing my dolls. I think it's safe to say that Boring Brian was *forced* by his mum to take Adam out with him, and by the looks of it, who could blame her. Even mums deserve time off for good behaviour.

Speaking of Mrs Pindar (and Mr Pindar), they're both looking slightly greyer around the edges than I remember them, and Brian's big sister Lynsey looks much the same, only bigger, being pregnant, but I wouldn't have recognized Adam at all; he used to be this pudgy little kid (not that I was a goddess or anything when I was little), and now he's ... just sort of nondescript. Skinnier, but nondescript. Apart from the fact that he still seems to be an idiot, of course; the pea-up-the-nose trick has been only one in a long line of stupid stunts he's pulled since we arrived. (His repertoire so far has included making farting noises when each of us came to sit down around the table, as well as singing "*Reach* for the spuds!!" really loudly when his mum put down a bowl of mash, which didn't even make Bethany giggle since she probably wasn't even *born* when S Club 7 had a hit with *Reach For The Stars.*)

"Now remind me; how long has it been since you two started going out?" asks Mrs Pindar, passing the dish of peas to Ruth, who takes it and very quickly passes it on.

(Something tells me no one's going to be in the mood for peas any more, having witnessed Adam's disgusting nose trick.)

"Eight years," Ruth replies cheerfully to Mrs Pindar's question, her neat brown bob bob-bobbing as she turns her head around.

"Actually, eight-and-a-half years next Tuesday!" Boring Brian points out.

Boy, that guy has too much time on his hands if he can waste it working out half-year anniversaries. . .

"Isn't that lovely!" Mrs Pindar twitters. "Just think – when you were both only twelve years old, holding hands, who'd have guessed that you'd be sitting here today planning your wedding!"

I'd have guessed – mainly because Ruth had come into my room on the very day she and Boring Brian had officially decided to be boyfriend and girlfriend and informed me that she was going to marry him. I was only six or seven and hadn't really figured out important stuff like the fact that you couldn't marry cartoon characters (I was madly in love with Aladdin from the Disney film at the time), but for all my ignorance, it still sounded to me like Ruth truly meant what she said. And to be fair, not one day has passed when she's thought any differently.

"And how long have you been married now, Lynsey?" my mum conversationally asks Boring Brian's big sister.

(My dad and Mr Pindar, I notice, aren't saying much of anything. Maybe it's just because they're busy getting stuck into the mounds of food on the table, and maybe it's because they think all this talk of weddings is women's work.)

"Four years," Lynsey replies smugly, patting at her large stomach.

27

(Out of the corner of my eye I'm sure I see Adam rolling his eyes and mouthing "four years" at the same time as his sister's talking.)

"It's a shame your husband's had to work today," says Mum. "We'd have loved to have met him, wouldn't we, Sean?"

Dad – caught out at being included in the conversation – starts to choke on his mouthful of broccoli. It's pretty funny, actually (well, it is once I see that he's not turning *blue*), and I almost can't hide my grin, until I spot Adam on the other side of the table, cackling away like he's watching an episode of *Only Fools And Horses* or something. He sees me clocking him and gives me a face-splitting grin – which I totally ignore. How dare he laugh at my poor old dad?

"Sorry, Lynsey. What were we saying?" Mum apologizes, as she finishes patting my dad on the back. "Oh, yes – your husband. What does he do that he has to work on Sundays?"

"He's a vicar," Adam chips in, his face super-serious now.

"Is he?" my mum answers, sounding very impressed, before Mr and Mrs Pindar, Boring Brian and Lynsey all yell "Adam!" indignantly at him.

"Ignore him," sighs Lynsey, giving Adam the evil eye. "My husband Barry works as an AA patrolman."

Adam is looking very pleased with himself for winding everyone up. My mum, on the other hand, just looks confused.

"So, he's not a vicar?" she repeats, trying to clarify what's going on.

In response, a lump of mashed potato lands splat on her chest, and dribbles down her best blouse.

"Bethany!" squeals Lynsey, grabbing a plastic Mickey Mouse spoon out of her giggling daughter's hand.

"*No!*" shrieks Bethany, trying to dig another dollop of mash before her missile-launcher is yanked from her hand. "Wanna do it again! *Again!*"

"Oh, Sheena – I'm so sorry!" Mrs Pindar apologizes, handing my mother a bundle of paper napkins.

"It's fine! It's nothing!" my mum shouts, above the ear-blasting screams of "AGAIN! AGAIN! *NOOOOO* – GIMME MY SPOON BACK!" coming from horror-child Bethany.

"Oh dear, oh dear," gabbles Mrs Pindar, rushing off to the kitchen to get something or other to make the mashed potato mess better (a cage for Bethany?).

"Are you OK, Mum?" Ruth asks, passing Mum another napkin.

"Yes, of course! Don't fuss! It'll come out in the wash, I'm sure," Mum says, sounding pretty dubious, as she dabs at the ever-expanding smear of tomato sauce in amongst the white potato sludge.

A beetroot-faced Bethany is now bucking violently away from her mum and screaming so hard that I'm worried the glass lampshade above the table will shatter over the uneaten peas. The dads don't seem to know what to say or do – same as me. What I really, *really* want to do this second (apart from not *be* here) is to find the volume control on Bethany and turn her down to zero.

And once again, I spot Adam grinning like a baboon (no offence to baboons, who are undoubtedly much nicer, smarter creatures than Adam Pindar).

Can I go home, please? Now?

The meal is over but the torture continues.

We're in the living room, all gathered around the telly as Mr Pindar plays us an ancient video of Ruth and Brian, aged about ten, running around the Pindars' (former) garden, playing tag. Honestly, *playing* tag might be fairly good fun, but *watching* twenty minutes of it isn't. So far, Brian's been "it" five times, while Ruth's been "it" four times. And that's about "it". The only diversion from this non-stop rollercoaster of fun is Bethany skipping back and forth in front of the TV yelling, "I'm it! I'm it! I'm it!" over and over again. (If "it" is an annoying little gremlin dressed up as a cute kid, then she definitely is "it".)

For a little while there, I tried to put myself into a calm, meditative trance and ignore my mind-numbing surroundings, but I couldn't – not with Adam sitting beside me making loud snoring noises till his mum told him to quit it. So instead, I let my thoughts wander to the phone call I'd taken just minutes before we had to leave for the Pindars today. It had been Jude, phoning to tell me it looked like it was all over between Molly and Nathan (actually, I think I was more surprised that the Molly/Nathan thing had lasted a whole three weeks rather than the fact that it was finished). Jude, Scott, Molly and Nathan had all been out the night before as a foursome (I had been invited to make it a fivesome, but the thought of spending time with muppets like Scott Mason and Nathan Blake made the idea of staying in and watching wall-to-wall quiz shows on telly with Mum and

Dad just *too* irresistible). Anyhow, they'd been out to see a movie, but when they went for a burger afterwards, Molly and Nathan had got into some big fight about –

Well, I never did get to find out what it was about 'cause Mum was hassling me to get off the phone and get in the car.

What was the argument about? Could it really (hopefully) spell the end of Molly and Nathan? And how long was it going to be before Jude wised up about Scott and I could get both my mates back again?

"Ooh! Look!"

"Ahhhh!"

"That's so cute!"

"Aw, bless!"

I'm vaguely aware of general cooing going on around me, and turn my eyes towards Bethany the Monster Child, presuming she's doing something adorable like dribbling out of the corner of her mouth or something to get all the adults going.

But it's got nothing to do with Bethany, who I notice is quietly sitting and playing nicely (for once) at the side of the TV.

"Oh, Shaunna!" sighs my mum, with that wobbly sound in her voice that I know from experience means she's got tears in her eyes. "Isn't that sweet! You must be about four there!"

I focus my wandering attention, like everyone else, on to the TV screen.

Urgh.

Oh, yes – that's me on the telly, aged four, wearing my favourite *Wombles* T-shirt, and with my hair (ruffled, as

31

usual) in two lop-sided bunches. I have absolutely no memory of being round at the Pindars being videod, and I certainly have no memory of letting a small, pudgy four-year-old boy try to snog me.

"Ahhh ... she's crying!" Ruth giggles. "You're crying, Shaunna!"

And it's true – even aged four I knew what I wanted when it came to boys, and evidently a snog from Adam Pindar definitely wasn't it, from the way I was bawling my eyes out as soon as his squidgy little lips locked on to my cheek.

"Hey, I don't *always* have that effect on women," Adam turns and grins at me.

I don't know what to say to that big-headed remark; I'm still in too much shock at having the toe-curling kiddie footage dragged out in front of everyone. And what suddenly shocks me now is realizing how horribly close Adam is sitting to me. The heat from his thigh feels like it's practically *burning* through my jeans. Instantly, I move my leg away, as if I've had an electric shock.

Coincidentally, I'm not the only one.

"Bethany – NO!" yells her mother, as all the adults in the room pounce on the Monster Child as she's spotted happily chewing her way through the TV cable.

Adam starts laughing until Brian lands him a whack on the shoulder, and he soon shuts grumpily up.

Lynsey yelps in pain as she bends over Bethany, and everyone gasps and assumes she's gone into premature labour or something, only from my angle I can see she's wincing from the bite her darling little devil-child has just given her.

Gosh, I haven't had this much fun since the time I went over the handlebars of my Barbie bike and chipped my front tooth.

Can I go home this time? *Please?!*

chapter four

All's fayre in love and weddings...

Date: *Saturday 13th April*

State of mind: *Devious*

Sightings of Star-Boy: *One! (Oh, deep joy and deep shame)*

I've had an excellent month. OK, not quite excellent (excellent would have to involve stuff like winning a life-time pass to *Top of the Pops*, or waking up one morning to find I'd been magically transformed into Penelope Cruz; that kind of thing), but it has definitely been good.

For a start, I had Molly back, safe from the clutches of Nathan Blake. Although she'd said nothing about it at the time ('cause she knew I'd tell her I-told-you-so) it turned out that her three-week relationship was as exhausting as being on an SAS training course. Constantly anticipating and wriggling free of advances of the octopus kind had made her very mentally and physically agile. Still, it hadn't made her mentally agile enough to recognize she should ditch the guy – that only happened the night of their fight, when Nathan told her she wasn't allowed to have chips with her burger, because he'd never be seen dead dating a girl who weighed over eight stone. At that point, a just-over-nine-stone Molly wised up quickly and told him where he could shove his chips. (Ouch – hope they didn't have vinegar on them. Then again, I do.)

"I should start a support group for all the girls who've gone out with the creep," Molly had suggested a couple of Saturday nights ago when she was round my house, slobbing out in front of a re-run of *When Harry Met Sally* on some cable channel. (We'd both seen it stupid amounts of times, but Molly in particular was up for cleansing her soul with a slab of great romance after surviving Nathan's less-than-romantic wandering hands.)

And so me and Molly (minus Jude for big chunks of the time thanks to her ongoing infatuation with Scott Mason) have been slobbing and shopping, and hanging out and having fun. Oh, and mooching about Westburn Park a lot. Y'know; just in case there's any sightings of a certain Star-Boy. . .

And apart from mooching with Molly, the other thing that's made this month pretty good is the fact that Ruth's been busy with a big, scary old work placement for college, which has kept her far too busy (er, make that traumatized) to go on too much about the W-word. God, it's been great not having conversations about fabric swatches and finger buffet menus and floral arrangements ricocheting about the house.

But of course, all good things must come to an end, and

so here we are: Ruth, Mum and me at the Riverside Hotel, gawping around along with a bunch of other brides-to-be, mums and bridesmaids at the finery on offer at the hotel's twice-yearly Wedding Fair. Oh, sorry – Wedding *Fayre*.

I think I've died and gone to cutesy hell.

I've never seen so much lace and fluffiness packed in one room. The word "wedding" is everywhere ("Wedding Album", "Wedding Invitation", "Wedding Place Cards", "Wedding Video Boxes", "The Wedding Etiquette Book", "The *How Weddings Turn Your Brain To Mush* Book"), all printed in swirly, twirly gold lettering beside bad drawings of fat cherubs, entwined hearts, church bells (moonlighting from their usual job as illustrations on the type of Christmas cards favoured by grannies) or doves.

The dove theme seems to have caught Ruth's eye. Who knows why, since doves are only pigeons that have been given a wash and blow-dry as far as I can see, and Ruth's been terrified of pigeons ever since the summer when one mistook her little toe for a piece of bread and pecked it. (She was eight. Ruth, that is – not the pigeon.) But having wedding fever seemed to have made my sister forget all that; right at this second she's cooing (sorry) over a row of strung-together white paper cut-outs that vaguely resemble birds, I suppose – if you squint hard enough.

"It's a garland of doves!" beams the stall-holder eagerly, her eyes shining in anticipation of flogging something that looks like a primary four art project for probably a "garland" of five pound notes.

"Isn't it beautiful, Shaunna?" Ruth sighs, holding part of the paper and string *thing* up for me to examine as if it were a piece of precious, antique silk.

"But Ruth, they're birds," I grin at her. "You don't *like* birds."

"Yes, but these aren't real," she laughs back blithely.

Oh, well, that's all right then. I know Ruth doesn't like snakes much either – so maybe I should suggest a "festoon" of rattlers weaving their way around the bride and groom's table at the reception.

"Ruth," I say (don't worry – I'm not *really* going to suggest snake decorations), "I just had an idea. Instead of this kind of stuff –" I try not to let my disgust creep into my voice as I point to the paper bird tat – "why don't you have something more arty?"

"Like what?" Ruth looks at me dubiously.

"Like ... like we could collect lots of branches with berries from Coldfall Woods a couple of days before the wedding," I suggest. "You could have bundles of them in the church, and then have them pinned up in, well, *garlands*, all around the reception, and even have small posies of them on each table..." I trail off, seeing that Ruth's expression isn't exactly spelling out enthusiasm for my idea.

"You could even spray them with a little silver paint, so they glitter, like they've got frost on them!" I chuck in, hoping the promise of a bit of twinkle will kick-start her imagination.

"Nice idea," says Ruth, in a tone of voice that means she thinks it's a rubbish idea but doesn't want to say it to my face. "But I don't really want something handmade on my wedding day, I want something special. Something –"

Mass-produced, I finished her sentence for her in my

head. *Something that's going to be seen at thousands of other copycat weddings up and down the country on that exact same day.*

But Ruth doesn't get a chance to tell me herself what her something special is – Mum is calling us over through the throng of women to a stall three up from where we are.

"Shaunna, sweetie, take those terrible clips out of your hair," Mum orders me cheerfully, before we've even squeezed through the crowds to her side.

I do as I'm told, reaching up and unfastening the multi-coloured plastic clips that I shoved randomly in my hair this morning to keep my growing-out fringe out of my face.

"Ta na!" Mum calls out, shoving something on my head before I've had a chance to see what it is. Whatever it is, it feels prickly, like a hedgehog's just parked itself on my scalp. Yeowww – I daren't move in case it embeds itself more deeply.

"Oh, Shaunna, look!" cries Ruth, holding up a hand mirror so I can check out the hedgehog on my head.

Only it's not a hedgehog. It's not as *tasteful* as a hedgehog. It's a towering bundle of plastic pearls, glitzy diamanté and trailing ribbonettes, all glued randomly on to a headband with vicious combs in it to keep it in place.

"It's called 'The Princessa Tiara'," says Mum, reading from the label that's dangling down by my cheek.

It sure doesn't make me feel like a Princessa. It makes me feel like moron. Princessa Morona. . .

For Ruth's sake, up until now I've been trying my best to act interested (and not aghast) at the avalanche of tweeness that we've walked into. Ever since we left the house, I've fixed Julia Roberts winning the Oscar in my head as an example of exuberance, and although I've got nowhere near that, I think I've seemed just about far enough on the right side of smiley to keep Mum and Ruth happy. But the indignity of having a tacky tiara foisted upon me in public is going too far. I feel like dumping down the piles of brochures Mum and Ruth have saddled me with and doing a runner.

Only I don't need to – I am saved by the bell. Or more precisely, the ringing tone. The strains of *I'm Just a Teenage Dirtbag, Baby* trill loudly from my mobile phone.

"Hello?" I say, as Mum retrieves the Princessa from my unappreciative head and puts it back beside its fellow naff tiara horrors. Only she is now trying to replace it with a circlet of artificial flowers (of no recognizable species), even though I've got a phone rammed against my ear.

The caller is Molly, and her desperate, tearful tones are loud enough even for Mum and Ruth to hear.

"It's OK, Mol – I'll be there as soon as I can!" I promise, after a few seconds' conversation.

"What's wrong?" Ruth asks, concerned, as I press the end call button.

"I don't know," I reply, looking from Ruth to my mum. "But she sounds in a bad way. Look, is it all right if I go and meet her; see what's up?"

"Of course! Go!" Ruth nods at me, and rubs my arm (for luck?).

"I hope she's OK!" Mum calls after me as I hurry away, waving back at them. "Oh, and Shaunna – Shaunna!"

It's a bit rotten to pretend that I can't hear Mum, but

I'm desperate. And two seconds later, I find myself scurrying away from the cloying, claustrophobic corniness of the fayre and stepping outside into the cool spring afternoon.

I've escaped. Molly's phone call was like a miracle. (Only it wasn't, but more of that later. . .)

"You should be taking a drama GCSE," I smile, slithering into a seat beside Molly in the busy shopping centre café. "You managed to sound really upset when you called!"

Molly raises her blonde head up and meets my gaze.

Yikes – if she's acting, then she deserves a leading role in the next Steven Spielberg movie. Her face is swollen with crying and her eyes are a deeply unhealthy vivid pink against her pale skin and hair.

"Oh, Shaunna!" she snivels, and it's only now I spot the clump (garland?) of damp, crumpled paper tissues spread out around her nearly empty cup of coffee.

"What's wrong?" I ask her, meaning it this time, whereas I hadn't when I spoke to her back at the Riverside Hotel.

The thing was, it wasn't a miracle that Molly had phoned me this afternoon – we'd planned her fake distress call as a way of getting me out of there after I'd spent a hopefully decent amount of time admiring embroidered wedding ring cushions or whatever. The miracle bit had been Molly's timing: she was supposed to phone me at half-three, but she'd called twenty minutes early, rescuing me just when I was most in need. Only it turned out that Molly wasn't faking it; *she* was in need too.

"Oh, Shaunna! He-he's been saying the most horrible things!" she hiccups.

"He who?" I frown, reaching over and grabbing some spare napkins from the neighbouring table. It looks like we're going to need them.

"Nath-Nath-Nathan!" she sobs. "He's been telling everyone!"

"Everyone like who?" I push her. "And what's he been telling them?"

"Everyone like Charlene Wilson and Sunita Patel," Molly sniffles into a tissue. "I saw them in TopShop earlier, and they said Nathan's been going around saying . . . saying I-I'm the three Fs!"

Molly looks shell-shocked, and I know I should too, only I haven't a clue what she means.

"What's the three Fs?" I frown.

"*Fat*," Molly spits out, "*frigid* and *ugly*."

"Ugly doesn't start with an F," I say, puzzled.

"It does when you put a swear-word in front of it," Molly replies, her eyes swimming in instant tears again.

Suddenly, my blood boils – how dare someone come out with vicious crap like that about my lovely friend, all because she wouldn't let him put his hand inside her Wonderbra? God, I could *kill* him! Or at least cheerfully trip him up next time I passed him in the corridor at school. But ranting about the unfairness of it all isn't going to make Molly feel any better.

"Yeah, but Mol – you have to remember that Nathan Blake is the three Ss," I tell her.

"What are they?" she asks, perking up a little now that I've got her curious.

"Well," I begin, counting off on my fingers, "he's slimy –"

That gets a flicker of a smile from Molly.

"– he's sleazy –"

Oh, yep – definitely a smile there.

"– and he's a total shi –"

But I don't get to finish my final S; my heart has just lurched from its normal position in my chest and lodged itself somewhere in my throat.

Two lads are weaving their way though the tables, laughing and chatting. They're about seventeen. The one in front is . . . well, I'm not even bothering to look at him, because the lad behind him is the one I've been day-dreaming (and night-dreaming) about for the last couple of months.

"It's Star-Boy!" I mumble in shock.

"Where?" Molly asks, and makes to turn around.

"Don't look!" I hiss at her, and Molly freezes, with only her eyes flicking wildly around in search of my love-god.

I can't quite believe I'm actually seeing him. I can't quite believe he's real. But under the unflattering, harsh mall lighting, he is – amazingly – taller, skinnier and even more beautiful than I remember him from that night in the park.

I want to stay in this second for as long as I can, freeze-framing his gorgeous face in my head, but I can't, because he's walking right this way, and I can't sit here staring at him like a love-sick Robbie Williams fan (even though there's nothing I'd like better).

Then, just as I'm about to divert my eyes, a truly *amazing* thing happens . . . as he walks towards us, he glances at our table, then at ME!!, and his Slavic cheekbones sharpen as he breaks into a broad, tooth-dazzling smile.

"Molly. . ." I force my voice to speak once he's safely passed. "That was him – the dark-haired one! And he *grinned* at me!"

Molly isn't reacting the way I'd expect her to; instead of looking pleased for me, she's biting her nails and wrinkling her nose nervously.

"Maybe he was grinning 'cause of those. . ." she suggests, stopping biting her nails to point at the array of wedding catalogues fanned out in front of me where I dropped them as soon as I'd sat down at the table.

Oh, God – how embarrassing that Star-Boy has seen me with these, like I'm some real saddo drooling my way through the pretty pictures of brides.

". . .or maybe it's that?" Molly cringes, pointing up at my head.

My heart has now left my throat and is sinking like a stone to the tiled café floor.

As I reach up with my fingers, I suddenly realize why Star-Boy was grinning. It's not every day you see a fifteen-year-old girl sitting in the shopping centre wearing jeans, a fleece and a flowery, peach bridesmaid's headdress.

Noooooooooooooooo. . .!

chapter five

Best man?
(Must be some mistake...)

Date: Saturday 11th May

State of mind: Vexed

Sightings of Star-Boy: I can count them on precisely *no* fingers

Scientists write papers on rare sightings of seldom-seen creatures, don't they? Well, I think in that case that I'm well qualified to write two papers; one on the Lesser-Spotted Star-Boy (no sightings since the floral headdress disaster four weeks ago), and the second on the fast-vanishing Bestus Friendicus (Jude variety).

It's crazy that Jude only lives across the road, and yet I've been seeing her less and less outside of school. Part of that is to do with exams (and studying for the rotten things), but Molly and me have still been able to find time to hang out and commiserate with each other on the sheer torture of swotting, with the aid of videos, ice cream and shopping, amongst other things.

Course the real reason me and Molly have been deserted is called Scott.

"Leave the girl alone!" my mum advised me, when I moaned to her about how invisible Jude's become in our lives. "She's in love! She's all starry-eyed! Let her enjoy it and she'll come back to you and Molly once the novelty's worn off!"

I didn't really like (or approve) of what Mum was telling me; we three – me, Molly and Jude – vowed long ago that boyfriends would never come between us, and while some people might argue that I'd never had a boyfriend so I don't know how hard it is to keep to that, I still think it's a valid vow. But, whether I liked or approved of it or not, I decided to take Mum's advice and not give Jude a hard time. Even when it felt like me and Molly had "second-best" stamped on our foreheads whenever Jude darted away from us in the school corridor to go and hang out with His Lordship, Scott.

Still, maybe the novelty *has* finally worn off. Jude (gasp!) called me this morning and asked if I fancied a wander round the shopping mall today. Shopping? I always fancied that. And since I also fancied Star-Boy and the only place I'd ever seen him apart from Westburn Park was our local, friendly mall, Jude could definitely count me in.

"Do you think Scott will like this?" asks Jude, holding up the sort of spangly boob tube I never thought she'd wear in a million years.

"I don't know," I reply non-committally, although I suspect it's *exactly* the sort of trash-sexy look Scott Mason would be into, going by the trash-sexy look girls he's dated

45

in the past. "What about this?"

I hold up a camouflage green, long-sleeved T-shirt with a red Buddha on the front – the very thing my skate-girl mate would have been dragging up to the cash-desk by now if her brain hadn't been sucked dry by a certain boy.

"Nah," Jude shakes her head. "Maybe if it was tighter, or cropped. . ."

Huh? Normally, Jude wore everything in a size "baggy".

"So, how are things going with Scott, anyway?" I ask, more out of politeness than genuine curiosity.

I know it might sound terrible, and like I'm not making any effort to get to know the guy my friend is so crazy about (crazy being the operative word), but you have to remember that Molly has seen Scott at close quarters (during her short-lived flingette with his mate Nathan), and reported back that although he isn't in the same sleazy, octopus-arm league as Nathan (thankfully) he is otherwise even worse than our not-very-flattering first impressions led us to believe. According to Molly, under that handsome exterior languishes the personality and sense of humour of a turnip (and somehow I don't think she means that as a compliment).

"Oh, Shaunna!" Jude suddenly says in this little-girl tone of voice that means it's time for me to stick on my Agony Aunt hat and get ready to dole out a few dollops of advice.

"What's up?" I ask, using the opportunity to wrench the hideous boob tube out of her hand and stuff it back on the rail.

"It's Scott . . . I'm sure he's going off me!"

Hallelujah! I'd rather see Jude chuck *him*, but since it

never happens that way round (Jude's never the chucker; always the chuckee), I'll just be happy to get her back to her senses, however that happens to come about.

"Why do you think he's going off you? Has he said something?"

"No – that's the trouble," Jude sighs, as we amble out of Miss Selfridge.

"You mean he's ignoring you?" I frown, trying to get a handle on her problem.

"It's not that exactly," she shakes her head. "It's just that when we're out, or when we're on the phone, I've just started to notice that it's always *me* who ends up doing all the talking. Scott just doesn't say anything much about . . . *anything*, really."

I want to yelp, "That's because he's a boring dork!", but I don't suppose that's too tactful – even if it is probably true.

"And last night, when I called him," Jude continues, "he kept yawning when I was speaking!"

The ignorant git.

"Listen, I'm *sure* it's not you," I begin, treading softly.

"But it must be!" she answers, fumbling about in her bag for one of her crisis cigarettes. "He's always got lots to say to his mates!"

I'm temporarily stumped. The thing is, Scott's a big oik and his friends are all big oiks, so Jude is hardly going to be missing out on any scintillating conversations. But how can I be honest with her without stomping all over her feelings?

"Listen," I shrug, as we're nearly mown down by a posse of mothers and baby buggies, "I know you don't want to hear this, but ... well, *maybe* the not-talking thing is because you and Scott don't, um, have *that* much in common."

There – was that tactful enough?

"But we do!" Jude protests. "I mean, when we kiss, it's *amazing*. It's just *so romantic. . .*"

I bite my lip and sneak a look at her. Jude is mightily in need of a dictionary, since she seems to be muddling up the concepts of "romance" and "lust".

"But the thing is, going out with someone – it's not all about the snogging part, is it?" I suggest, fanning her horrible trail of smoke away from my face. "You've got to have stuff to talk about, as well as having a laugh together, haven't you? That's all part of romance too!"

Jude stops dead and shoots me a look that makes me realize that somehow I'm not saying what she wanted me to say. I think I was just supposed to sympathize and tell her that having a silent, yawning, uninteresting and uninterested boyfriend is perfectly normal.

"Shaunna, you really think you know everything, don't you!" Jude snaps at me suddenly, which seems pretty unfair really, considering she *asked* for my opinion. "You're as bad as Helen! *She's* got a downer on me and Scott too!"

Wow – I'm quite honoured to think I have something in common with Jude's very cool mother.

"But the funny thing is," Jude rants on, "my dad dumped *her*, and you've never even *had* a boyfriend, but you *both* think you know what's best for me!"

OK, this is getting silly. I can tell that Jude is feeling very fragile, seeing as she probably knows herself that this thing with Scott is fizzling out faster than a squib in a hailstorm, but she doesn't have to be so snippy.

"Jude! That's *so* not fair! All I'm trying to say is—"

"No – *you* don't understand," she interrupts me, all indignant and upset. "Scott is the cutest-looking guy at school – he could go out with anyone, but he chose *me*. And I don't want to lose him!"

That's the dumbest reasoning I've ever heard. But I'm not about to hear anything else from Jude right now – she's just gone stomping off and left me standing like a complete pillock in a fug of her stinky smoke.

Well, while *she* goes off and tries to think up topics of conversation to fill the silences between her and Scott, *I'm* going to go home for a relaxing afternoon.

A relaxing afternoon of moping miserably about the house and moaning down the phone to Molly about how hurt I am. . .

Except that's not what's happened.

I didn't get the chance to do any sorry-for-myself moping. I'm now sitting in a breezy pub garden (I'll explain in a minute), having just spent the afternoon checking out potential wedding reception venues with Ruth. And while that would normally sound about as tempting a thing to do as having my toenails ripped off with pliers, it was actually pretty good fun. Well, anything would be fun after the business of Jude going all stroppy on me this morning.

It happened like this: as soon as I got home from the mall, Ruth pounced on me, begging me to help her out. Mum was actually her number one venue-checking buddy (since Boring Brian was working), but a small emergency of the granny kind had sent Mum scurrying off to the other end of town. Our Granny McKay is a fiercely independent (and fiercely fierce) old Scottish woman who is hell-bent on doing all manner of DIY herself, no matter how many ulcers it gives my mum and dad. This time, it seems, she'd been using a blowtorch to strip the paintwork around her kitchen window and managed to lightly char her curtains into the bargain. As always (touch wood), no harm had come to her (only, in this case, the curtains), but Mum felt duty-bound to go over with a copy of the Yellow Pages and sort out a professional painter for Granny before she incinerated the rest of her flat, as well as the neighbours'.

And so I found myself in Ruth's battered old Nova, zipping from one snoot hotel to another; Ruth having a good time being chaperoned around swanky function suites by ingratiating managers, and me having a good time, well, in a quite different way. . .

"Oh, the Haslemere was gorgeous, Brian!" Ruth sighs over the splintery picnic table that our empty glasses are perched on.

(It's six o'clock, we've just met up with Brian, and we're in the breezy beer garden of the Swan pub. We're not allowed actually *in* the Swan pub because of me – being only fifteen, we're relegated to the outdoor – and out-of-season – family area.)

"Wasn't the Haslemere gorgeous, Shaunna?" Ruth smiles at me, tucking her neat brown hair neatly behind her neat little ears. "Weren't those long, rose-coloured velvet curtains beautiful?"

I nod enthusiastically, but what I immediately think of when she mentions the Haslemere is the manageress twittering on about the bewildering "package" options Ruth could choose from. Apparently, she could go for Package A or B (X amount of guests plus Y amount of time, times Z amount of decorations), and then choose between Menus A, B or C (with X equalling prawn cocktail starters and Y equalling trifle or something). It ended up sounding like an algebra lesson, and maths was never Ruth's strong point. No wonder she just ended up drifting off and gazing at the nice curtains.

"But then the Crescent Hotel was lovely too," Ruth tells Brian, wafting a brochure under his nose.

"Hmmm!" Brian mumbles, raising his eyebrows in excitement. (Well, I suppose it's excitement – I've never really seen Boring Brian get excited about anything very much really.)

"The Crescent had the most *amazing* food," Ruth enthuses, producing a sample menu from her bag and adding it to the pile of literature for Brian to inspect.

"Yeah, the most amazing food, if you like salmonella!" I laugh, suddenly remembering what we saw when the kitchen doors swung open. I'm sure it's not in the chef's rule book that you pick up the bit of chicken you just dropped on the floor and shove it in the wok anyway. At least, looking at the manager's shocked face I guessed it wasn't.

"Oh, I'm sure that was a one-off! Just a little mistake!" says Ruth, thinking – as she always does – the best of people and situations. The mug.

"Well, if you have your wedding at the Crescent, then I'm *definitely* taking my own lunchbox!" I tease her, while Brian grins away.

(Brian: I've never described Brian properly. So to set the record straight, Brian is . . . Brian is beige. He's got beige hair – always moussed flat – beige skin and a beige personality. I don't mean to be horrible, but he really never has an opinion on anything. Or *says* anything. I mean, he's kind of sweet, in a gerbil-y way, but let's face it – he's not Mr Rock'n'Roll. By a *loooonnnngggg* shot.)

"Well, I thought the Crescent was lovely," Ruth exclaims, from some weird sense of fairness, "but it doesn't matter, because. . ."

Drum roll, please. Ruth is pulling out her final brochure and has a *This Is It!* grin plastered across her face.

". . .Brian – I think this is the one for us!"

"Yeah?" says Brian, raising his eyebrows enthusiastically towards his prematurely receding hairline.

"Yeah!" Ruth murmurs breathlessly. "The Regency – ooh, it was just fantastic, wasn't it, Shaunna? It has the most *amazing* gardens that would be *perfect* for the wedding photos. And then the bridal suite! That brass bed was just the *best* thing. But no – you know the best thing? The absolute best thing? Well, when it comes to the meal, they don't just give you the three courses – oh, no. They only go and throw in a white chocolate, shaped like a dove, with the coffees, and they do that for free! And then there's the –"

Oops! I've tuned out. Ruth is about to go into full-scale prattle about the wonders of the Regency and its particular wedding package, and as nice a time as I've had this afternoon (specially sniggering silently at the very posh Regency manager's squint wig), there's only so much wedding detail I can take in before I go numb.

But it's funny, I think, while I stare at (but don't listen to) Ruth and Brian's one-sided conversation. *This is a bit like what Jude was saying this morning. About her doing all the talking. . .*

God, is it always like this with boys? Them giving up trying when you're together? Trying to talk, I mean? OK, so it's different when you compare Jude's boyfriend to Ruth's: Scott Mason is horrible and Boring Brian is at least smiley and sweet. And even if Brian never says much, at least he seems totally fascinated by whatever *pearls* fall out of my sister's mouth. Brian would never, I repeat *never*, yawn when his beloved was talking. Even if she was wittering on about different types of bread rolls, like Ruth is doing right now. . .

"Do you think wholemeal, or white? Or a mixture of the two?"

Please – Brian's brain might not be melting but *mine* is.

"OK!" booms a voice. "Pint for Bri! Gin and tonic for the lady! Only kidding, Ruth – orange juice; I know you're driving! And a large whisky for the little lady! Only kidding! Coke for you, Donna!"

"Shaunna," I correct Brian's work buddy Wayne, who's come along with Brian tonight after the store closed, for no apparent reason, other than to make bad jokes and get my name wrong. Or maybe that's a bad joke too.

"Thanks, mate!" says Brian, clinking his glass against Wayne's as he steps into the picnic table seat and settles down.

"Brian!" Ruth suddenly whispers urgently, grinning and shooting her boyfriend a knowing look. "Tell her!"

I'm not sure what's going on here. I glance from Ruth, to

Brian, to Wayne (who, incidentally looks exactly like Brian, down to the mousse-flattened hair, apart from the addition of a criminally awful moustache), but I'm still none the wiser.

"Uh, Shaunna," Boring Brian smiles at me. "This is Wayne."

"I know," I shrug.

We were introduced earlier when Ruth (and me) drove up to the industrial estate and picked both the guys up.

"Yeah, but the thing is, Shaunna, Wayne is going to be my Best Man!" Brian announces, patting a jubilant, hairy-upper-lipped Wayne on the back.

Best Man.

Best Man. . .

There are plenty of people out there in the world that could be described as Best Men. Maybe Bono, for the work he's done for the reduction of debt in the Third World. Or Nelson Mandela, for being . . . well, Nelson Mandela. Or maybe Bob Geldof, for helping feed people who'd been forgotten by their own governments. Or even Star-Boy, for being so beautiful (and only grinning and not *sneering* at me for looking like a geek that day in the mall).

OK, so Star-Boy might not be so worthy of being called a Best Man as the others, but he still has that certain some-thing *wondrous* about him, which Wayne – a moustachioed electrical salesman with a crap sense of humour – does not.

But at least I can be thankful for something; at least I'm not going to have to stare across the aisle next February at geeky Adam, who I'd half suspected would be Brian's Best Man, seeing as he's his brother and everything.

"Cheers! Look forward to a bit of slow-dancing with you on the big day, Donna!" says Wayne, taking a sip from his pint glass of Guinness and then clanking it against my half-pint of Coke.

I check out the wodge of unpleasant, creamy foam that's dangling from Wayne's moustache and sigh – very quietly, very sadly and very much to myself – as I remember the time when Molly and Jude joked about the possibility of me and the Best Man falling for each other.

Compared to the only boy I'm interested in, Wayne comes out spectacularly badly on first sight. The only Stars *he* looks at are probably the ones you buy at the newsagent, with page threes in them. . .

chapter six

Gurgle, gurgle, hurl...

Date: *Sunday 23rd June*

State of mind: *Back-to-front*

Sightings of Star-Boy: *One, by proxy (boo)*

"Shaunna! It's me!" squeals a high-pitched voice down the phone.

The "me" is Molly. And in the background I can hear more squealing, which sounds suspiciously like Jude. And I can also make out a male voice, which – if I'm not mistaken – belongs to the lead singer bloke out of the Stereophonics.

"What's up?" I ask, as I cradle the phone under my chin and crouch down to finish fastening up my new shoes, while nodding my head up and down in time to the distant music playing behind Molly and Jude.

(At that point Dad nearly trips over me, scurrying

about under Mum's orders as we all faff about in readiness to leave the house.)

"You'll never believe it!" Molly giggles hysterically. "Me and Jude – we're in HMV!"

Wow – my two best friends are spending their Sunday afternoon moseying around a record shop. Incredible! Next thing Molly will tell me is that they might stop off for a *coffee* somewhere afterwards. Wild!

"Uh-huh?" I frown down the phone. "You're in HMV? So what?"

Any other time, I'd be more than happy to yak away about nothing very much with Molly and Jude (in fact that's one of my favourite things ever), but right now my mother is twirling around the house like a hormonal tornado, desperate to see the family all decked out in our finery and get us to the church on time.

"He's *here*, Shaunna! That *boy*!" Molly shrills.

The world is full of boys. Loads of them. She's going to have to be a bit more specific than that.

"Who are you talking ab—"

"Shaunna! Come *on*!" Mum hurries me, holding the front door open and ushering my dad and Ruth out like she's a fire-drill monitor.

"Oof, gimme the phone!" I hear Jude say, and there's a rustling and a giggling as the mobile gets passed between her and Molly.

"Listen," comes Jude's voice, "it's him – Star-Boy! I'm looking over at him right now! He's in the Hip-Hop section with a couple of mates!"

If today wasn't today; if my legs hadn't just turned to jelly; and if I was wearing my trainers instead of these girly wedge shoes, I could run out the front door right now and be in HMV in twenty minutes. Fifteen if I really hammered it. And knowing how long boys like to slouch around in record shops, there was still a chance that Star-Boy would be there, letting his heaven-gazing eyes drift around the Soul section (what else).

But today was today, and I have to leave for a sodding christening right now. In fact, *sooner* than right now, by the looks of Mum, who is stomping towards me and reaching out to grab the phone.

"Got to go! Watch him for me! Bye!" I say hurriedly and slam the phone down before I suffer the total shame of having my mum yank the receiver away from me and tell the girls I can't talk any more.

"Right, can we actually go now, Shaunna?" Mum sighs at me, stress adding an edge of sarcasm to her voice. "Or is there anything else you want to do?"

"Yeah," I mumble as I head out of the door in my uncomfortable shoes. "Shoot myself. . ."

"Thanks *so* much for inviting us to the christening today, Lynsey. We're all *so* honoured to have been there!"

Speak for yourself, Mum.

"It was lovely to have you," beams Boring Brian's sister Lynsey, hugging a bale of white broderie anglaise to her bosom. (All that's visible of her new-ish baby is one tiny wiggling finger, signalling to the world that he's still alive after the trauma of being half-drowned in a font and smothered by a froth of lace.)

"Isn't the church beautiful, Sheena?" Brian and Lynsey's mum comments, all misty-eyed. "I'm so glad you had a chance to see it before the wedding!"

"Oh, so am I, Mary – I can just picture our Ruth gliding down the aisle now. . ."

I'm standing here in Mrs Pindar's front room, nibbling politely on a bit of dry sponge cake, wishing I could work out a way to disengage myself from the dullest conversation in the world. Not that my chances of finding a decent conversation anywhere else in the house are looking too good, since it's packed full of unknown Pindar & Co. relatives in smart suits and posh frocks, nearly all of them ancient. I think it's safe to say that I've got more chance of snogging Star-Boy than finding anyone fun to talk to this afternoon. Might as well go and lock myself in the toilet now. . .

"The whole *thing* was beautiful," Mrs Pindar twitters endlessly on. "And ickle Frankie was an angel!"

Well, yes he was – until the vicar dared to dribble water on his head and then he screamed so much he was sick, I think to myself.

"Oh, yes! Wasn't he!" my mum agrees with Mrs Pindar, trying not to drop any of her cake on the ground as a small, thigh-high gremlin runs screaming and shoving past her. Bethany, I notice, hasn't suffered in any way from nearly being electrocuted last time I saw her, when we were round at the Pindars for Sunday lunch (make that Sunday torture) a few months ago.

Boring Brian's sister is, of course, looking quite different – mainly because "ickle Frankie" has made his entrance into the world. And since it was his christening today, I hold this snoozling, milk-drooling little bundle responsible for ruining my chances of ever getting to know Star-Boy. If it wasn't for ickle Frankie, I could by now be talking love, life, the universe and hip-hop with my star-gazing love-god. Well, probably not. But at least I'd have got a fix of staring at him. That would be enough to keep me going for *weeks*. Actually come to think of it, I should have told Jude to go and buy one of those throwaway cameras, so her and Molly could try and snap a photo of Star-Boy as they trailed him. At least then I'd have something concrete to lust over, instead of relying on a hazy memory. Or maybe I could turn detective myself, trawling the city, showing his photo to strangers in the hope that someone, somewhere knows *something* about him. (His name? His phone number? His star sign? Hey, even just his *shoe* size would give me a kick at the moment.)

"Ow!" a male voice suddenly gasps behind me, right before I feel the dull thud of someone's elbow on my back that sends my sponge cake flying into orbit (or at least on to the carpet at the other side of the room).

"Sorry!" says someone, grabbing my arm, and steadying himself and/or me.

"Sowwy!" mumbles another voice, and me and the someone holding my elbow turn to see Adam Pindar give us an apologetic shrug as he continues chasing Bethany through the throng of legs.

Adam looks somehow . . . *weird* today, I think, squinting to figure out what's different. Then I realize it's because he's got cheesy footballs crammed in his mouth, racked up in a row like mutant monster teeth. Yuck.

"Did he just bump into you?" I ask the boy who's holding my elbow, focusing for the first time on a nice face, with nice freckles and thick, thick eyelashes.

Behind me, I can hear the mums (including Lynsey) tut-tutting over Adam getting Bethany "over-excited".

"Nah – it wasn't Adam," the friendly-looking, freckly boy shakes his head. "It was –" he pauses and glances over at Lynsey, before dropping his voice – "it was Bethany. She's got this new trick of kicking people in the back of the knees, 'cause it makes them fall over. Hilarious, huh?"

"Ah!" I mumble back, picturing Bethany skipping about during the christening, and suddenly realizing what had caused the unexplained groans and yelps I'd heard during the service.

"Yeah, and I think Adam's just trying to distract her," the boy with the freckles continues, nodding his head in the direction of Bethany's giggles and shrieks just now.

"Omigod, and she's going to be the flowergirl at my sister's wedding. . ." I whisper, becoming horribly aware that part of my duties as bridesmaid will be having to physically restrain Bethany from causing mayhem and misery on the Big Day.

"Oh, so you're Ruth's sister?" says the boy with a certain amount of surprise in his voice.

I raise my eyebrows, daring him to explain himself. What's so surprising about me and Ruth being sisters? Is it a shock to find out that neat and delicate Ruth is related to scruffy me? (Even though I started out pretty neat myself today, I'm starting to feel my hair wriggling free of the slides I clipped it back with, and I've been fidgeting around with my new shirt 'cause it's too tight under the arms. I'm *sure* I've got damp patches. Urgh. . .) And how does this boy know Ruth anyway?

61

"I'm Dean," says Dean, beaming so that the freckles on his nose disappear into crinkly smile lines. "I'm Brian's cousin. And Lynsey's and Adam's, of course."

"I'm Shaunna," I reply, finding myself smiling shyly all of a sudden. "So you've met my sister already?"

"Yeah, a couple of times. I can see the resemblance now," he says, narrowing his eyes at me and grinning. "You're both . . . girls."

Funny. Pretty funny, freckly boy.

"So will you be coming to the wedding, then?" I smile at him.

"I hope so. I don't just want to get invited to christenings. They're a lot less fun than weddings, and there's a lot less free booze. . ."

He *is* quite funny, this cousin of the Pindars'. Who'd have thought that there'd be someone this promising in the family, when you considered the blandness of Brian, the mumsiness of Lynsey and the annoyance of Adam?

"Speaking of booze, I think I know where there's a bottle of cider. D'you want me to sneak you a glass?" he tempts me.

"Go on, then," I laugh.

Well, it's a better offer than more dry cake and cups of over-milky tea. But speaking of sneaking around, another thought suddenly strikes me.

"Dean," I whisper, grabbing his sleeve before he slopes off, "where's the phone? I really need to make a quick call and I haven't brought my mobile. . ."

"It's just out in the hall," he points. "Don't worry – Auntie Mary won't mind."

But what *I* mind is the thought of anyone listening in,

so when I get to the phone, I practically push myself backwards into the mountain of jackets dangling from the coat rack.

"Molly?" I whisper, when I hear a scratchy hello.

"No, it's me, Jude," says Jude. "We're in Westburn Park – Molly's just gone to buy us a couple of ice creams."

"Is *he* there?" I ask, my heart leaping, since I'll forever link Westburn Park with my first significant sighting of Star-Boy.

"Nah, we lost him – him and his mates left HMV while we were queuing to pay for this two CDs for a tenner offer," Jude explains. "I'm really sorry, Shaunna. . ."

And she *does* sound sorry, which is as sweet as her sounding excited for me earlier, when her and Mol rang to tell me how they'd spotted Star-Boy. It's sweet 'cause Jude and I have come to a bit of an understanding over the last few weeks (ever since she blew up at me): the deal is that *Jude* doesn't go on about Scott in front of me (oh, yes, they're *still* together and no, I *still* don't approve of him) and in return *I* don't go on to her about Star-Boy (since she doesn't approve of me fantasizing about unobtainable boys, as she so bluntly puts it).

"That's OK," I assure her, feeling a flutter of disappointment, but not really expecting anything else.

"Anyway, how's it going there? Has that christening thing been a real bore?"

If Jude had asked me that five minutes earlier, I'd be making a low groaning noise at this point. But five minutes can make a lot of difference. . .

"No, it's OK, actually," I grin to myself. "I'll tell you more later."

"Ooh, sounds interesting!"

"Well, maybe it is and maybe it isn't!" I laugh. "Listen – I'd better go. Bye!"

Jude would be pretty proud of me if she knew the thoughts that are currently skittering their way around my mind. Stuff like ... well, maybe that she's right; maybe it *is* stupid to hanker after a boy I've seen two-and-a-half times in five months (I count Molly and Jude's effort today as a half). And maybe it *is* time I looked for Close-To-Home-Boys instead of Star-Boys.

After only five minutes and a stare at his freckles, I can't say Dean is definitely someone I could fall for (he didn't make my heart go *ping!* at first sight the way Star-Boy did), but Molly and Jude might have a point – I should give people (boys) more of a chance. And here comes that chance now. . .

"There you go," grins Dean, walking through a door that came directly from the kitchen and handing me a paper cup fizzing with bubbles.

"Thanks!" I say, taking the cup and taking another peek at Dean while I'm at it. He's about the same height as me, maybe the same age as me, maybe a little bit older (and maybe it's just the black suit he's wearing that makes him look older). He's built like a rugby player (fit but kind of stocky), which isn't the type I go for at all (I tend to like lads who come in either scruffy, skinny or Star-Boy varieties). But there's something very kind about his eyes and from the crinkle lines on his nose, he does a lot of smiling, which can't be a bad thing.

"So did you have fun today?" Dean asks me, working those crinkle lines.

"Maybe it would have been more fun if I didn't feel like such a fraud," I reply, keeping my voice low. "I mean, I hardly know Lynsey. And since I only saw him from the back, I still don't even know which bloke is her husband!"

"Hey, listen – *I* know a lot of people here, and trust me, it doesn't make it any more fun," he laughs softly. "So what would you have been doing today if your family hadn't been invited along?"

Ooh, he didn't want to know.

"Um, just hanging out with my two mates," I shrug, telling the truth (but not the whole truth).

"Yeah – my mates were going to the movies this afternoon; they're showing a special re-run of *The Matrix*. I love that film," he says wistfully.

"I remember seeing that ages ago, when it came out on video."

"On video? Nah – you've *got* to see it on the big screen!" he enthuses.

"Have I?" I laugh.

"Yes! The special effects don't look half as good on the telly."

"Wow – I thought they were pretty good when I watched it on vid."

"Honestly, seeing it on the big screen would blow you away!"

"Would it?"

"Definitely. You've got to catch it. And it's only on for the next couple of days."

"Hmm, maybe," I shrug. "If I can find someone to. . ."

Go with. That's the end of the sentence, but I can't say it. It would sound too much like I'm hinting when I'm not – it's just that Jude and Molly hate sci-fi stuff, even if it does have the added attraction of Keanu Reeves.

Then I notice that me and Dean are looking shyly at each other, silent and in suspended animation, both of us sensing where the conversation is potentially going and neither of us knowing what to do about it. Then, bless him, Dean speaks.

"So how about it?"

"How about what?" I smile, knowing exactly what he means, but just wanting to double-check I've got this right.

"How about coming to see it with me?"

So, I *didn't* get it wrong. I have – drum roll, please – just been asked out. On a date.

"OK," I shrug, hoping I don't sound too surprised.

Hey, Jude really *will* be proud of me now.

"Woo-OOO-ooo!" comes a strange noise from directly above us, spoiling the moment.

Me and Dean both glance up, and see Adam leaning over the banister at us, while Bethany grins through the bars like a demented high security prisoner.

"My cousin's not hitting on you, is he, Shaunna?" Adam grins, revealing no cheesy footballs this time but some horribly orange gungy teeth. There's also a pretty rank cheesy smell wafting around as he talks too.

"*No,*" I say firmly, trying not to breathe through my nose. "He is *not* hitting on me."

"Hmm, didn't sound like that from where I'm standing!" Adam continues to tease us. "What do you think, Beth?"

Adam and Bethany exchange wicked glances, which makes me and Dean exchange embarrassed ones.

"*Deanno and Shaunna up a tree!*" Adam suddenly breaks into song, only to be joined by Bethany for a rousing chorus of, "*K.I.S.S.I.N.G!*"

I'm so mortified I could do an ickle Frankie and hurl on the spot. As my face flares up like a furnace, I really feel like P.U.N.C.H.I.N.G. Adam Cheesy-breath Pindar. . .

chapter seven

Apricot meringue?
No thanks.

Date:	Monday 22nd July
State of mind:	Stuffed with fluff
Sightings of Star-Boy:	None – too busy with my boyfriend to go searching

"Shaunna!" squeals Ruth, clapping her hands when I come out of the cubicle. "You look like . . . like something out of Cinderella!"

"What – the pumpkin?" I ask, staring at my vaguely orange, puffball reflection in the mirrored wall.

It's Ruth's lunch-hour from her summer job in Next, and we're presently in a wedding "boutique" called Bella Bella. (Which always makes me think of *Pizza Bella*; "Could I have the Margherita dress with an extra topping of hand-embroidered netting, please?")

"No, not like the pumpkin," Ruth giggles, bending down and brushing a non-existent thread off one of the ruffles on the voluminous skirt of the dress I'm wearing. "Like *Cinderella* out of Cinderella! When she went to the ball!"

That's bad news. If I look like Ms Cinders *after* she spruced herself up for the posh dance, then it must mean that I look like a street urchin the rest of the time.

I gaze over my shoulder longingly at my rumpled T-shirt, faded denim skirt and pink flip-flops back in the cubicle. The sales assistant notices, but misinterprets what I'm doing.

"Hold on – I'll get the perfect one for you!" she beams, trotting over to the display of tiaras and headdresses that's parked on the left-hand side of the changing rooms. Uh-oh – I sense a case of déjà-vu. . .

"Oh, *yes*!" nods Ruth, as the sales assistant gingerly places a beribboned, befeathered, floral extravaganza on my bonce. "Shaunna, check yourself out!"

I *am* checking myself out. The headdress perfectly tops off a dress that consists of so many layers and details that it might well have been welded together from five different dresses. Altogether, I look like a victim of a hit-and-run by a bunch of five-year-olds armed with a dressing-up box.

Ruth's wedding day is Ruth's wedding day, but I've got to put my foot (currently wearing a peach satin ballet pump) down. I can't be seen in public looking like a cross between a pumpkin and a doily. I'd have to leave town.

"The thing is, I just don't think I really suit orange," I whimper.

"It's not orange! It's apricot!" says Ruth brightly, still giving the dress a worryingly approving glance-over.

"Well, I don't think I really suit apricot, then," I correct

69

myself. "What about that blue one over there? Can I try that?"

The deep blue dress I'm pointing to on the rail is *still* not very me, but it does have the advantage of being a) blue and not apricot, and b) plain and straight rather than as wide as the Millennium Dome.

"It has to be apricot, though, Shaunna, 'cause that's the colour of my bouquet!"

"Can't you have some blue flowers in your bouquet instead?" I suggest, in desperation.

"You don't *get* blue flowers, Shaunna!" Ruth giggles good-naturedly.

"Yes, you do!" I insist, then remember I'm thinking of the weird dyed blue chrysanthemums you sometimes see flopping limply in buckets in petrol station forecourts. And I don't suppose Ruth will be nipping into the local Texaco on the way to the altar next Valentine's Day.

"Honestly, if Dean could see you now. . ." Ruth sighs happily.

Dean.

If Dean could see me now he'd tell me I looked . . . nice. And then wink at me to let me know he wasn't being entirely serious. I could rely on Dean not to snigger at my expense. As boyfriends go (judging by my mates' experiences, since I've nothing to compare him to) he's a bit of a gem.

So why aren't I falling in love with him? Why does nothing tingle and nothing turn to jelly when he kisses me? Not that it isn't nice kissing him. But that's the trouble – Dean is a nice boy; kissing him is nice; we have a nice time when we go out. Everything is nice, but in the ten dates we've had since we met, I've never been hit with the sledgehammer of longing to see him, or felt the *twang!* of Cupid's arrow when he leaves me. And if romance hasn't reared its head after ten dates then I don't suppose it's going to happen – not when I felt an instant zap within ten seconds of spotting Star-Boy that very first time in the park.

But maybe I'm being stupid. Dean is a really . . . nice (oh dear) guy. Everyone likes him, not just me – Molly and Jude are part of his fan club, not to mention the whole of my family. Maybe I've got to be patient. Just like there's falling in love at first sight, maybe there's falling in love at eleventh sight or something. . .

"Pppppppppffffffffffff-*wa-HA*!"

Whatever that is, it's not a very appropriate noise for the serene, fluffy world of Bella Bella. The sales assistant is frowning very hard at the perpetrator of the horrible exploding snigger, and I turn round too, making my headdress topple to one side so that it dangles unflatteringly over one ear.

It's at this rakish angle that I spy – even though the vision in one eye is obscured by apricot feathers – Adam Pindar in the doorway, pointing and laughing out loud at *me*.

"*Aaaaaaaaaaaarrrrrrgghhhhhhhhhhhh!*"

From somewhere behind his knees, a small, shouting torpedo hurtles into the shop and fires itself directly at Ruth, who nearly topples off at the direct hit.

"Hello, Bethany!" she smiles once she's got her breath and her balance back. "Thanks for bringing her, Adam! Oh –" she pauses, turning to the still-startled looking sales assistant – "it's all right, they're with me!"

The sales assistant doesn't look too reassured. Bethany, her face covered in a liberal smearing of ice cream, sticks her tongue out at the woman.

"Bethany here is going to be my flowergirl," Ruth explains. "Aren't you, sweetie?"

"*Aaaaaaaaaaaarrrrrrrgghhhhhhhhhhhh!*"

"So we'll need to find a – *oof!* – a dress for her too!" says Ruth, while trying to stop the dungareed, sticky-handed gremlin from clambering on a white satin chair, and getting an accidental kick in the stomach for her trouble.

Now the sales assistant really *doesn't* look too happy.

"Shall we perhaps pay a quick visit to the bathroom to wash your hands?" she mutters dubiously, as she ushers Ruth and a wildly bouncing Bethany through to the back of the shop.

"Hope they've got a lasso in here," Adam sniggers, as they disappear from view.

"A lasso?" I frown at him, finally straightening my hideous headdress in a vain attempt to hold on to a shred of dignity.

"Yeah – tying Bethany up is the only way they're going to keep her still enough to get her into a frock!"

He's probably right, but I don't feel like agreeing with him – he's not my favourite person in the world, and there's nothing worse than someone you don't particularly like seeing you at your most vulnerable – ie, in a ridiculous apricot meringue.

"Excuse me, I've got to get out of this," I mutter, flouncing off (which is very easy to do in this particular dress, since it's made up almost entirely of random flounces).

But there's still no escaping Adam. Even in the relative sanctuary of the changing cubicle, I can hear his voice drifting through the curtain.

"So that, um, *dress* . . . is that definitely what you're going to be wearing for the wedding, then?" he bellows.

I can practically *hear* the smirk on his face (if that's possible).

"Not necessarily," I shout back, as I wrestle to get my hand far enough around to grab at the zip.

(By the way, by "not necessarily", I mean – of course – "not if I can help it. . .")

"Aww, I can't *wait* for the big day," Adam bellows back, his voice wobbling as he tries not to laugh at his own jokes. "You and Dean are going to make such a *lovely* couple!"

As I shake off the rustling meringue, I end up staring at my reflection in the mirror (I should have at least worn matching knickers and bra today, street urchin that I am).

Standing frozen like that – with the stupid feathery, flowery headdress still plonked on my head – Adam's words ring in my ears, and I suddenly realize that I'm finding it hard to picture myself being with Dean next *week*, never mind next Valentine's Day.

True romance – it still seems as far away as . . . well, as the stars. (No guesses who *I'm* still dreaming about. . .)

chapter eight

*Just close friends,
family and everyone
we've ever met...*

Date: *Sunday 18th August*

State of mind: *Flabbergasted*

**Sightings of
Star-Boy:** *A 100% close-up! (Almost...)*

This is weird – I can hear raised voices in the living room. We may be a pretty ordinary family, but in our house, you're about as likely to hear raised voices as you are to hear my dad cranking up UK Garage tracks on a mixing desk.

"What's going on?" I ask, sticking my head around the living room door.

Ruth, Boring Brian and Mum are all sitting around the table, while Granny is parked in an armchair, busily polishing a pair of brass candlesticks that normally sit on the fireplace. I wonder if this is the source of whatever's caused the raised voices; Granny finds it impossible to sit still (in other people's houses as well as her own) and is forever cleaning things that don't need to be cleaned when she comes round to ours. It really winds my mum up – she's always wrestling cans of Mr Sheen and Brillo pads out of Granny's hands and trying to make her drink tea and eat biscuits like normal visiting grandmothers.

But judging by everyone's expressions, it doesn't look like Mum could care less what Granny wants to polish today – there's obviously a bigger battle of wills going on, and it's between Ruth and Boring Brian. . .

"What's going on is stupid guest lists," Ruth whimpers at me, slapping her hands down flat on several scribbled-on sheets of A4 paper.

"Now, now, Ruth, I'm sure you can find a way of sorting all this out," Mum says soothingly, in her best peacemaker voice.

Somehow – probably I'm guessing from the killer sideways look Ruth's just given him – it would seem that Brian has done a Very Bad Thing. And my mission is to find out what that Very Bad Thing is without starting off World War III again.

"What's the problem?" I try to ask nonchalantly, as I lean in the doorway (I don't want to get any further into the room in case I get dragged into something I'll regret).

"We can have a hundred people at the church, and another fifty at the reception," Ruth says in a flat, fatalistic tone.

"So?" I frown.

"So Ruth's done a list of who should come and there's three-hundred and sixty people on it so far," Boring Brian explains.

"Well, *you* do it, if you're so clever!" growls Ruth, slapping the scrawled list of names in front of him.

"Aw, c'mon! Don't be like that!" replies Brian, who looks hurt, but just a little bit annoyed too.

This is getting weirder. I've never seen Ruth and Brian get grumpy with each other. *Ever*. And here they are getting grumpy over wedding plans, when getting married is the one thing they're supposed to be *dying* to do. I dunno; it just shows you that weddings aren't about romance; they're about lists and planning and organization and *stress*.

"Give it here," says Mum, reaching over and grabbing the reams of names. "Let me see . . . let me see. . ."

She's scanning down the page, tapping a pen against each name.

"Malcolm and Kirsty? Why have you put them down?" she quizzes Ruth.

I strain to place faces to those names, and eventually remember that Malcolm is an older cousin of my mum's who I've met once, when we were on holiday in Scotland and hooked up with some of the extended family. And if I've got this right, he was with a woman whose accent was such a thick Glaswegian that we all needed an interpreter – she must have been his wife Kirsty.

"Well, Mum, when you were away making tea, Granny said we'd *have* to invite them because you were the bridesmaid at *their* wedding," Ruth explains.

"I was their *flowergirl*, and I was *four*," Mum points out, shooting a glance at my frenetically polishing gran. "And I've only seen them a few times over the years since. Anyway, there's no point in inviting them; they divorced in 1992."

"Did they? I don't remember that!" says Granny in surprise, her own, perfectly translatable Scottish accent sing-songing. "Well, you'll just have to invite them both, with their new partners, if they have them."

"No, we won't," says Mum firmly, crossing a line through the names, while Granny tuts under her breath. "And who's this here?"

I can't resist going over and peering over Mum's shoulder at the A4 sheets. It seems that Granny was pretty helpful while my mum was out of the room; adding a whole pile of people to the list who nobody in my family has heard of/who nobody in my family is speaking to/or who are dead. Still, Mum's doing a neat job of weeding them all out and hacking the list down to more sizeable proportions.

"There we go – that's a start!" Mum says brightly, tossing the paper and pen back over to Ruth and Brian. "Now you two have a go at paring down the list!"

"Well, since Mum's cut loads from *our* side, *you'll* have to take a turn," Ruth says to Brian, sounding a bit petulant.

"But Brian's only written down about twenty names altogether!" I can't help laughing. "All the hundreds of others are on your side!"

"Thank you, Shaunna, but I don't think you appreciate how much work a wedding is!" Ruth snaps at me.

"And I don't think you realize that getting married is supposed to be an expression of love, not planned out like a military operation!" I snap back, hurt that Ruth seems to be taking out her stress on me.

All I see is four shocked faces as I storm from the room, grab my bag and head out of the front door.

Leaving the house wasn't as dramatic a gesture as it sounds. I did have somewhere to go: Westburn Park, as it happens.

And here I am now, with a huddle of mates, sitting on a rug Jude's dragged from her house, and tearing open family-size bags of crisps. It's not any old sunny, summer afternoon in the park; there's a charity rock concert going on (oh boy, Jude's neighbours are going to have a field day writing in to the local paper, moaning about decibels and litter and whatever), and the place is heaving. There are hundreds and hundreds of people lying about on the grass in the sunshine, chatting or staring aimlessly at the stage and listening to the bands playing. Not that there's anyone famous in the line-up – just a bunch of local bands – but I'm not complaining. It's the most exciting thing that's happened round here in ages, and I'm in serious need of getting cheered up after all the petty flipping-out going on back at my place...

"Shaunna? Want some?" asks Dean, wafting a two-litre bottle of Coke in front of my face.

Oh, yes. We're still together. And no, I'm still not in love.

"No, that's OK," I shake my head, and point to the can of Lilt I've just opened.

Dean shrugs with a smile and instead fills up the empty plastic cup that Molly's holding out to him.

So why haven't I finished with him yet? Well, it's Dean's own fault, isn't it? For being so unremittingly nice and not giving me one good reason to chuck him. I mean, if he had a habit of picking at spots in public, or wearing old-man-style nylon socks, or making borderline sexist jokes, then it would be easy to dip out of this. But the way things are, what do I say? "You're really nice; you're cute-looking; I like your company . . . but I'm finishing with you"? It just doesn't sound convincing, does it? "Tell him you just want to be friends," said Mum, when I picked her brains about it (although I can tell she's faintly disappointed with me for not seeing the loveliness of Dean, which she most certainly has succumbed to). But that's so lame too, isn't it? And it sounds like a total lie – as if what you really mean is "I'm just letting you down gently – please never phone or talk to me again."

God, I wish Jude would tell Scott Mason that she only wants to be friends. But fat chance of that happening, the way she's sitting, nuzzling up to him right now.

"I thought you were playing in some league match today, Scott?" I say to him, hoping I sound like I'm trying to make an effort to be sociable, although I know it probably sounds more like I'm saying, "Why are you here, spoiling our afternoon, Scott?" Which, of course, *is* what I'm thinking.

"Scott got hurt," Jude starts to explain, animatedly. "Someone tripped him up in yesterday's match and –"

"I got *injured*," Scott corrects her wearily. "I got a bad *tackle*."

Jude simpers a bit and has this apologetic, I'm-just-a-silly-little-girl look on her face. I wish she wouldn't do that.

"But I thought you'd want to go down and support the other lads in your team," I continue, knowing that it still sounds like "Why are you here, spoiling our afternoon, Scott?" but I can't help it.

"Nah – it'd wind me up too much, seeing them play without me. And anyway, if you're not playing, what's the point, really?" Scott announces, showing himself up as the selfish, self-centred git I'd always taken him for.

"But it's great you could come along to this instead," Jude tells him, wrapping her arm around Scott's waist.

Scott acts like he hasn't even heard her talk, let alone acknowledging her hug, and turns his attention to Dean, who as the only other male in the group is obviously the only person worthy of connecting with. I can't bear to make eye contact with Jude, and instead swap a tiny, uh-oh glance with Molly.

"So what kind of music are you into?" Scott asks Dean.

"Loads of stuff," Dean replies enthusiastically, since he has no real idea how obnoxious Scott is. "But my favourite band is Radiohead."

"Crap!" snorts Scott, sniggering at Dean's choice.

"Nah! They're brilliant!" says Dean, rising good-naturedly to the challenge.

Honestly, I can't be good-natured around an ignorant, testosterone-fuelled entity like Scott without suffering serious brain damage. I know it's mean to leave Dean with him, but he's a big lad and able to look after himself.

"Fancy checking out that henna tattoo place?" I ask Molly and Jude, nodding over in the direction of the bundle of rickety wooden stalls and tents set up over by the bandstand, where a variety of cooking smells and bright-coloured crafty items vie for the attention of the audience's senses.

"Sure!" says Molly, tucking her blonde hair behind her ears and jumping to her feet.

"Nah," says Jude, shaking her head and cuddling in closer to Scott, even though he seems about as aware of her as a tick on a water buffalo.

"It's not just me, is it?" I whisper to Molly, as we begin excusing ourselves and stepping over people's legs to get out of the lounging throng.

"You mean, Scott?" Molly whispers back, following right behind me. "No – it's not just you. He *is* a pig."

"It's just the way he treats her – I can't stand it!" I tell Molly, letting my voice rise to a normal pitch now that we're far enough away from Jude, Scott and Dean.

"And the way Jude acts when she's around him; she totally changes!" Molly moans.

And it's not just the way Jude turns into a twittering, pathetic wimp in front of Scott – it's the way she's changing her looks too, which must be to please him. Her short crop? She's growing that out, and she's had these really naff wide, blonde streaks put in her dark hair. Maybe that suits some people, but Jude's got this peachy-pink skin which clashes horribly with those bad, yellowy highlights. And now she's started staggering around in these terrible high-heeled strappy sandals that she can't walk in. We were running for the bus the other day, and by the time me and Molly were gasping and paying the driver for our tickets, Jude was still clacking along about half a mile down the road. We had to get off and wait with her for the next bus.

"How can Jude stand it?" I shake my head, as we reach the edge of the sitting crowd, and suddenly hit a wall of people, mooching back and forth between the delights of the snack bars and beer tents. "I mean, she's read books; she's seen movies; she knows what romance is supposed to be like. She's *got* to realize that her relationship is rubbish!"

"I know!" Molly agrees, struggling to stay close to me as an army of bodies jostle us about. "The thing is, she's only got to look at you and Dean to see what it's like to have a *proper* boyfriend; someone who really cares about you and –"

Oh . . . my . . . God.

I caught a glimpse of HIM just now – over by the beer tent. He's out of view just as quickly, 'cause of all the heads and shoulders blocking my way, but it was *definitely* him.

"Mol!" I squeak, interrupting whatever she's saying. "It's Star-Boy!"

Molly squints in the direction I'm peering in, then glances back at me. She seems to be frowning.

"Who cares?" she asks me.

"*I* care!" I laugh, feeling my heart race in a way it hasn't done for months.

"But you've got *Dean*!" she stuns me by saying. It's like, how can she even compare them?

"But this is Star-Boy!" I try to explain. "I've got to try and catch up with him! This could be my big chance!"

I start walking, changing my direction from the route we were taking towards the henna tattoo stall and heading instead towards the crush of the beer tent.

"Coming?" I grin excitedly at Molly over my shoulder.

"No," says Molly, straight-faced, standing her ground.

"Oh, come on, Mol! You've got to understand!" I plead with her.

"No – I'm going back to the others."

My stomach twists into an uncomfortable knot at the note of disapproval in her voice.

"Please yourself," I say sadly, "but I'm going to look for him."

"And what am I supposed to tell Dean?" she asks, as people buffet her from all sides.

"I – I don't know," I shrug uselessly.

Molly shoots me a look that makes me feel like I'm a bride who's ditching my fiancé at the altar, which is ridiculous. I mean, I *like* Dean, but I've never felt as strongly about *anyone* as I have about Star-Boy – that feeling when your heart is horribly, *brilliantly* raw and tender; when your bones *ache* at the very thought of someone. I've got to try and follow this through. That's what love's all about, isn't it? No one can be angry with you for trying to follow your heart. . .

But Molly's doing a pretty good job of being angry right now, and she's off – turning and disappearing into the mass. I turn myself in the opposite direction, wishing Molly hadn't spoiled this for me. Well, *nearly* spoiled it. I can't stay hurt and concerned over her attitude when I'm now staring at the vision before me . . . Star-Boy, standing with mates, staring towards the stage, pushing his dark hair off his forehead as he watches the musicians with the same earnest concentration as he watched the stars that first night I saw him.

I'm getting closer, and I temporarily lose sight of him as people get in my way – then there he is again, his face cracking into a wide smile at something someone's said to him, those cheekbones sharp, angular and lightly tanned.

I have no idea what to do once I get closer up; no idea how I can possibly get talking to him, but I've got to try. Maybe if I just stand near him and watch the band, nod my head in time a little, let him see I'm a music fan same as him. If he sees me, I'm bound to know ... I'll feel his eyes boring into me, and I'll turn and give him the smallest, shyest smile, nothing pushy. Then maybe he'll smile back, letting me see that killer grin close up again, like the time in the café at the mall. And then maybe –

Maybe nothing.

As I wriggle my way towards Star-Boy and my destiny, things go suddenly, hideously wrong. Right beside me, there's shouting, roaring, arms flailing as a drunken fight breaks out. One minute I'm clocking it all, trying to side-step quickly out of the way; next thing I'm on the ground, being used as a crash mat for a boozy-smelling lad who has just taken a punch from some other boozy-smelling lad.

As a sea of faces stare down at me on the ground, I wonder faintly if I'm paralysed – I can't move my legs at all. But as hands come down and pull the leaden weight of a six-foot bloke off me, I feel instantly weightless, as if I could fly away.

Maybe I'm concussed, not paralysed. . .

"Jeez, Keith, you idiot! You nearly flattened that girl!" I hear a disconnected voice say somewhere above me, and vaguely notice someone yelling at the guy who squashed me.

I'm starting to feel stupid – everyone is staring at me,

but no one is helping me, and I don't think I've got the energy to get myself up.

"Sorry," says the guy who is Keith, leaning over me alarmingly and breathing beery fumes down into my face.

"Let her get some air!" says the voice who was shouting at Keith, and another figure lunges down towards me, this time thankfully not smelling too boozy. "Come on, I'll give you a hand – shit, it's Shaunna! Shaunna?"

It takes a bit of effort to get my eyes in focus, but when I do, the view isn't too tremendous. . .

"Sorry, that was just my mates Keith and Greg," says Adam Pindar, putting his arm around my waist and hauling me to a standing position. "They always end up battering each other when they get their hands on anything to drink. The rest of the time they're best buddies."

I'm only half-listening; now that I'm upright, I'm scanning around in a panic for Star-Boy, but he's gone, probably moved off when he saw the drongos nearby breaking into a fight. I feel such a huge wave of disappointment that my legs almost crumple underneath me.

"Hey, are you OK?" Adam's voice grates in my ear, as he steadies me again.

OK? I think numbly. *OK is definitely what I am not, and that's got nothing to do with the fact that my ribs feel as bent out of shape as wire coathangers. . .*

I'm close enough to see that Jude is smoking – a sure sign that things aren't going fantastically well for her this afternoon. She's still got one arm draped around Scott, but he's leaning forward, staring at the stage, as if he's trying to move as far away from her as possible.

By contrast, Molly and Dean are chatting and laughing.

Has she told him? I wonder, getting ever nearer to my friends.

Has she told him I scampered off in hot pursuit of the boy I've had a mad crush on for the last six months? Whatever – I don't know how I'm going to explain where I've been for the best part of an hour. Searched for Star-Boy ... got caught up in a fight ... searched some more for Star-Boy ... gave up... I can't come out with something that brutal in front of Dean, even if it is the truth.

Oops. I feel myself flushing as Dean spots me and waves. Well, at least that smile of his tells me that Molly kept my secret to herself, no matter how much she doesn't approve.

As I tentatively wave back, I realize that Dean is too nice a person to string along like this. The thing is, even if Molly hasn't exactly made me feel that way today, *I'm* a nice person too – and I know that however horrible it's going to be, I've *got* to let Dean go. . .

chapter nine

Can I have a toaster, a loo brush and a big bust-up, please?

Date: Sunday 1st September

State of mind: Bamboozled

Sightings of Star-Boy: Back to zero

"Have you two ever heard of wedding lists?" I ask Jude and Molly, who are lounging, as usual on a boring Sunday afternoon, on my bedroom floor.

Molly looks up from a magazine, Jude stops examining the lyric booklet in her new CD, and they both nod at me.

"Course," says Jude. "*Everyone* has them when they get married."

Wow – how did I miss this? I'd never heard of a wedding list till an hour ago, when I saw Ruth downstairs, ticking her way through some brochure from Debenhams or John Lewis or some other big store. It's just that – call me naïve – but I thought people who come to your wedding know you well enough to buy you nice gifts that they're sure you'll love and cherish. (OK, so doddery old relatives might need a little inspiration, but they can always call your mother up or something, can't they?) But I tell you, it's come as a real shock to find out that you're supposed to celebrate a couple's love by looking at a shopping list they've given you, and deciding between buying them the Morphy Richards Four-Slice Toaster or an antique-pine loo brush.

Y'know, the more I find out about the mechanics of weddings, the infinitely less romantic they get. . .

"I just couldn't be that mercenary – insisting that people buy me stuff off some list!" I frown, stretching out on my bed.

"Yeah, but everyone gives hints about what they want for their Christmas and birthdays, don't they?" says Molly. "So what's the difference?"

"The difference is that it's just *hints*," I point out. "I mean, it's my birthday soon, but it's not like I'll be handing you and Jude a typed-up list of presents I expect you to buy me!"

"True. . ." Molly shrugs in agreement, and looks back down at her magazine.

"You know, I hate all this materialistic stuff about weddings," I moan on. "What's a toaster got to do with true love?"

"Not much," Jude agrees. "So you wouldn't have a wedding list, then?"

"I won't ever have a *wedding*!" I announce. "Nope, when me and Star-Boy get together –" I can see Jude and Molly rolling their eyes, but they know I'm only fooling around –

"we'll just live together, in a little, ramshackle cottage by the sea, with roses from the garden stuffed into old jam jars and homemade bread on our big, old, second-hand kitchen table. . ."

"Oh, yeah?" grins Jude. "And how are you and your live-in lover going to toast your homemade bread if you haven't got a Morphy Richards Four-Slice Toaster?"

That deserves a pillow in the face, and I instantly chuck one at her. I'm laughing, Jude's laughing, but I notice Molly most certainly isn't. Actually, Molly hasn't done much laughing at all recently – not around me anyway, and not since I finished with Dean. I know she didn't approve of me chucking him, but this frosty-faced stuff she's been giving me lately is starting to upset me a bit.

I mean, it's not like it was easy, finishing with Dean. In fact, it makes me cringe when I remember how it happened. I did the deed the night of the concert in Westburn Park; asked him back to mine for a coffee, thinking I could get it over with in the privacy of my room, over a couple of Digestives. I just hadn't figured on Boring Brian being round at ours, and as soon as we got in the door, Dean was corralled by his cousin and my dad into watching some stupid football match on TV between The Congo and Tasmania or somewhere. I ended up sitting next to Dean on the sofa, listening to Mum fussing over him with extra cushions and offers of all-butter shortbread, while I bit my nails down to my wrists with nerves.

In the end, it was awful – Brian announced he'd give Dean a lift home, so I had precisely as long as it took Ruth's darling fiancé to have a wee and find his car keys to bare my soul to Dean.

"Listen," I blurted out, as the two of us waited out on the pavement beside Boring Brian's boring old Volvo. "I've got something to say!"

"Yeah?" Dean grinned at me.

"Yeah. Um . . . Dean, you're great. Really great. And funny. And sweet too. You're . . . you're like, the *nicest* boy I know. . ."

I was wittering, I knew, but I couldn't seem to stop with the roll-call of his virtues and get on with the nasty blunt truth bit. Not that I needed to; with every compliment I gave him, Dean's smile faded a little. He has another virtue that I hadn't got round to mentioning – he's smart, too, and right then he knew that there was a great, big "but" coming any second.

"Ah, it's like that, is it?" he interrupted me, with a sad smile on his face. He looked like a trusting puppy who didn't understand why his owner was stuffing him in a cardboard box and dumping him outside the RSPCA shelter.

"Oh, Dean – I'm sorry!" I whimpered, hiding my bright red face in my clammy hands.

He didn't say anything else – there was a commotion at the door as Brian came out in a hail of goodbyes from Ruth and my mum.

"Can we still be friends?" I whispered before he got in the car, and immediately regretted how corny it sounded.

Dean slid into the passenger seat and gave me another soulful, dog-eyed stare.

"Sure," he shrugged, and then pulled the door shut.

"Sure," as in "No way – not after you just chucked me." I haven't heard from him or seen him since, and Brian hasn't been much help; all he told me when I asked how Dean was was, "Fine, I suppose," and that was that. So now, in the eyes of my entire family (and Molly), I'm just a shade more heartless and evil than Cruella De Vil. At least that's how I feel. . .

"Well, if me and Scott ever get married," Jude trills away, hugging the chucked pillow and still caught up in our previous conversation, "I think I'll have my wedding list at Thornton's! Then I'll never have to buy chocolate again!"

"You are joking, aren't you?" I giggle, and try and push the hideous image of Jude and Scott getting married to the back of my mind. "The way *you* get through chocolate, Jude, it wouldn't even last till the end of the honeymoon!"

I'm just dodging the pillow that's flying back in my direction, when I suddenly hear some kind of kerfuffle going on outside on the stairs.

"What's that?" frowns Molly, looking at the closed bedroom door and the direction of the sounds.

"Don't know. . ." I mumble, pushing myself up off the bed and going off to investigate.

Just as I open my bedroom door, I hear Ruth's – right next to mine – slam shut. I can also hear sobbing.

"She's crying!" I mouth to my friends. "I'd better go and check on her!"

And so I pull my bedroom door closed and tap gently on Ruth's.

"It's me. . ." I mumble hesitantly, pushing the door open a crack.

My sister is on the bed, looking unusually rumpled in her very unrumpled, Next-decorated room.

She gives me a silent, watery-eyed glance, but doesn't tell me to go away.

"What's wrong?" I ask, hurrying over to the bed and sitting down beside her.

It makes me feel slightly sick to see her so upset – Ruth's natural state is to be forever smiling, even when (especially when) she's nervous.

"Oh, Shaunna! It's all off!" she sobs, mashing a defenceless paper tissue up in her hands.

"What's off?" I ask stupidly. What did I *think* was off – the telly? The dishwasher? It can only be one thing, but surely she can't mean the wedding. . .

"The wedding!" she sniffles, confirming my worst fears.

"But why?"

Did Boring Brian actually have a wild streak? Had she found out that he was living a double life, with a wife and six children hidden away somewhere? But secret wives apart, what terrible thing could have happened to split up the happiest, most compatible couple I know?

"B-Brian. He – he. . ." Ruth stumbles over her words.

I give her hand a squeeze and wait till she's able to compose herself.

"His – his *parents* –"

She was hiccuping with tears. My God – what had Mr and Mrs Pindar gone and done?

"Ruth! Ruth!" Mum's voice calls out, as I hear her thundering up the stairs and rushing into my sister's room. "I just got off the phone – Brian's really upset; he says he'll get everything sorted out. He'll make sure you get the Zanussi!"

"It's too late!" Ruth gulps. "How can I trust him when

he was standing up for his parents, and not *me*?"

"Mum?" I squeak, fixing her with a questioning look. I haven't the *tiniest* idea what's going on here.

"Ruth put a washer/dryer on the wedding list," Mum explains, settling herself down on the other side of Ruth and wrapping her arms protectively around her. "Brian's parents said they'd get it for them, but that they'd only get a Hotpoint."

I'm still frowning. I am still lost.

"But Ruth has her heart set on a Zanussi," Mum whispers to me.

I can't believe it. My sister has just broken off her wedding because of a brand of washing machine?

"It's not the Zanussi! It's the *principle*!" Ruth sniffles, as she buries her head in Mum's chest. "Brian sided with *them* over *me*!"

"Ah, right. . ." I mumble, patting Ruth on the arm, and slowly getting up. "I'll, uh, leave you to it, Mum. . ."

Mum gives me a wave with one hand as the other strokes my sister's tear-soaked hair from her face.

Gently, I close Ruth's door behind me and find myself back in the sane world again.

"What's wrong?" Jude asks, as I walk back into my own room.

"Brian and Ruth are fighting over stuff on that sodding wedding list," I sigh, not even bothering to add that the wedding's supposedly "off". I can't believe anything that stupid is really going to split them up.

But even though my brain's a bit scrambled at the lunacy I've just witnessed, I find another thought pinging into my head.

"Where's Molly?" I ask.

"Loo," says Jude.

Right – maybe this is my chance; maybe Jude will know why Molly's giving me the cold shoulder.

"Jude. . ." I begin, settling myself cross-legged on the floor beside her. "Do you know what's up with Molly? I seem to be really bugging her somehow."

Jude bites her lip, then shoots a look in the direction of the hall, as if she's checking for signs of Molly's return.

"Shaunna, it's about Dean," she whispers.

"Yeah, I know she thinks I was mad to dump him, but you can't go out with someone if you don't fancy them, can you?" I try to defend myself.

"It's not *that*," Jude whispers again. "It's just that Molly . . . well, Molly really likes him. I mean, really, *really* likes him."

"What?" I yelp. "Molly fancies *Dean*?!"

"Yep – she's fancied him since you first introduced us to him," Jude enlightens me further. "And she just can't believe you treated him so badly."

"I *didn't* treat him badly! She's only thinking that way 'cause she likes him so much!" I protest. "Anyway, why didn't she tell me how she felt, once we'd broken up?"

"'Cause . . . well, 'cause going after your friend's ex. . ." says Jude, wrinkling her nose up, "It's a bit creepy, isn't it?"

"What's creepy?" asks Molly, who is now standing in the doorway, with a tense expression on her face that makes me think she's heard more than that last smidgen of me and Jude's conversation.

There's only one thing to do. I bound to my feet and walk towards her. Molly looks panicky, as if she thinks I'm about to slap her or scream in her face or something.

"Molly," I say, standing right in front of her. "I would love, love, *love* for you and Dean to go out, if that's what you both want!"

Now she looks like she doesn't know whether to laugh or cry with relief, and to be honest, neither do I. I didn't want to lose a boyfriend and lose a best friend into the bargain.

"C'mere!" I grin, giving my number one mate (not counting Jude) a big hug.

"Oh, Shaunna!" Molly snuffles into my shoulder.

What a weirdly emotional afternoon this is turning out to be. Ruth's blubbing, Molly's blubbing, and I'm on the verge of blubbing. I turn my head slightly just to check that it's not contagious and that Jude's not joining in with the blub-fest.

Thankfully, she seems dry-eyed.

Funny that; if any of us have got a genuine reason to cry it's *her*, considering the big, useless lump she's going out with. . .

chapter ten

The best part of breaking up is the making up

Date: *Saturday 7th September*

State of mind: *Cunning*

Sightings of Star-Boy: *Too busy being cunning to go Star-Boy spotting*

Here's a game no one's playing in my house: Happy Families.

For the last week, Ruth has been doing some top-class moping, staring at the phone in between sobbing sessions, as if she's willing Brian to ring, and then when he does, refusing point-blank to talk to him.

It's the same when he's come round the house; Mum's had to turn him away and say that Ruth doesn't want to see him, which is *hugely* hard for Mum considering she thinks of Brian as a son already. Dad's miserable too – it's difficult for him at the best of times to be outnumbered by three women in the house, but when there's so much emotion flying around, he doesn't know what to do for the best. When he's at home, he's spending most of the time hiding behind the newspaper, tutting sadly.

Me? Well, I can't help but soak up some of the misery, even if I do think that it might be self-inflicted. . . Not that I'd say that to Ruth. Right now she needs to feel like we're all on her side, and hopefully she'll be able to see things a bit clearer soon.

Hopefully.

But something tells me she's already feeling like she's overreacted to the Hotpoint fiasco, because she keeps coming out with new faults she's miraculously found in Brian: stuff to do with him not taking enough interest in the wedding – that sort of thing. Again, I wouldn't tell her, but I'm kind of on Brian's side there. I mean, it's hard to get excited about which metallic finish to get your wedding meal place-cards edged in, isn't it?

So anyway, from last Sunday to last night, the four of us have mooched around the House of Gloom; no one sure how to make things better. Then last night, something happened that might just change everything round. And then again it might not – it does involve Adam Pindar after all, and normally I wouldn't trust him to put a model plane together (he'd probably weld bits of it to a Sindy doll to get a cheap laugh), never mind putting a broken romance back together again.

But hey; no one else has come up with any ideas on how to end the stalemate. And so when Adam called me on my mobile (he got the number off Dean) and came up with his proposition, all I could say was yes, no matter what reservations I had. And *still* have. . .

"Shaunna! What are you doing here?" says Ruth, pausing as she potters around the clothes on the rails and arches her eyebrows at me in surprise.

It's five to six on Saturday, I've just walked into Next, and I'm about to put Stage One of Adam Pindar's plan into action. (God help me. . .)

"I – I just thought I'd come and meet you from work," I shrug, forcing my features into what – hopefully – looks like a sad expression.

(On an industrial estate a mile down the road, Adam should be saying and doing exactly the same thing. If he doesn't blow it by sniggering, of course.)

"Is something wrong?" Ruth frowns at me.

The other girls in the shop seem to be tidying up suspiciously tidy-looking clothes rails very close to us all of a sudden. They must be anticipating another chapter in Ruth's wedding drama. I was sure she wouldn't have been able to resist spilling the beans to her friends over the tea break.

"It's just that I really need to talk to someone," I mutter, casting my eyes down at the carpet. "Could we go for a coffee once you've finished up?"

"Of course!" says Ruth, her eyes full of concern. "Give me ten minutes – I'll meet you at the back entrance, yeah?"

I nod, and mumble what I hope sounds like a heartfelt "OK. Thanks, Ruth."

Wow – who knew I could act so well? And who knew the first part of Adam's plan would actually work? Still, there're two more stages to go; *plenty* of time to mess up. . .

"But I thought you didn't fancy him!" says Ruth, gazing questioningly at me over her foamy cappuccino.

"Well, that's what I thought too, till I saw him and Molly . . . y'know, *together* the other day," I shrug unhappily.

Oh yes, this is Stage Two, and it involves more acting. We're now in a cosy, old-fashioned, red vinyl booth in the Singing Kettle Coffee Shop (where no one's ever heard a singing kettle, but who cares about details when the place sells the best chocolate doughnuts in town). I'm now pouring out my heart about how much I regret chucking Dean, which is my contribution to Adam's plan.

("But how am I supposed to get Ruth to come with me to the Singing Kettle?" I asked Adam last night, when he spelled out his idea for getting Ruth and Brian back within talking distance again. "*I* dunno!" he'd replied. "Tell her you want to talk to her about how hacked off you are that you're not going to be a bridesmaid any more!" Ha – I didn't think my acting skills were good enough to pull off a whopper like *that*. And so, I've come up with the Dean storyline. I only hope Adam turns up with Boring Brian soon, before I have to do something drastic like turn on the waterworks to keep Ruth hooked. . .)

"Oh, poor Shaunna!" sighs Ruth, reaching across the formica table and covering one of my hands with her own. "Your ex-boyfriend and your best mate! That must be *so* hard!"

Well, I don't suppose it's going to be so much hard as awkward, when I finally *do* see them together. And I *will* see them together at some point, 'cause Molly wasted absolutely no time getting in touch with Dean after I gave her the green light. In fact, she phoned him that very afternoon, from my house, from my mobile, and with my blessing. They've seen each other twice so far this week already, and Molly seems blissfully happy. By the sounds of it, I'm *sure* the two of them are going to be a whole lot better at the boyfriend/girlfriend thing than me and Dean ever were. Not that I'm going to tell *Ruth* that.

"Yeah, I just feel so gutted," I lie, hiding my face in my hands, since I'm not sure I can *do* "gutted". Maybe you need to go to drama school for complicated emotional stuff like that. I'm suddenly realizing my limitations as an actress; I guess I'm more school nativity level than Royal Shakespeare Company.

I wish Adam and Brian would hurry up.

"It's a pity me and Brian, aren't . . . still . . . well. . ." Ruth startles me by saying.

"What?" I ask, dropping my hands and staring at her. "You mean, you want him back?!"

"No! Oh, no!" Ruth shakes her head in alarm. "Don't get me wrong! I just meant, if we were still together, I could have got Brian to have a word with Dean – y'know, tell him how you feel!"

What I feel right now is panic. Over Ruth's shoulder, I can see Adam walk in, with a startled-looking Brian in tow. And from what Ruth's just said, this is all going to come as a bit of an unwelcome shock, rather than a heart-warming surprise. . .

Still, Stage Three is about to happen, and there's nothing for it but to give it a whirl. Even if I *am* risking my sister excommunicating me from the family after this.

"Yeah, well, I've just got to nip to the loo. Back in a sec,"

I mumble to Ruth, slipping out of the booth and giving Adam and Brian a fleeting glance as I do.

Jeez – Brian's looking terrible. Even the quickest peek at his gaunt face and the bags under his eyes shows that he hasn't done anything that resembles eating or sleeping in the last few days. He almost looks as bad as Ruth, whose eyes have been so permanently red-rimmed and blood-shot recently that our neighbour asked if she had conjunctivitis. And Brian seems uncomfortable too – now that he's spotted Ruth, he's trying desperately to back-pedal, but Adam's grabbed hold of him and is pro-pelling him towards an unsuspecting and oblivious Ruth.

OK – I'm out of here; I can't stand to watch the carnage. . .

The ladies' loo of the Singing Kettle is decorated in two styles: old lady cuteness (lacy curtains; dusty plastic flow-ers in an old fashioned vase; Glade air freshener) and years-old scuzzyness (peeling paintwork; luminously green limescale in the sink; piles of greasy-looking fluff in the corners of the cubicles).

I gaze around after I've washed my hands and wonder how this place escapes the wrath of the Environmental Health inspectors. Not that I *want* it to close down; the Singing Kettle is a bit of an institution in town – my mum and dad used to come here on dates when they were teenagers. Actually, maybe the Environmental Health people have a soft spot for it, too – either that or the old couple who run the place bribe them with unlimited chocolate doughnuts and cappuccinos. . .

Anyway, I know I'm just dawdling – trying desperately

not to go back out there and see what's gone on. Will Brian and Ruth be talking? Or will the booth be empty, with only the indentation of a chucked sugarbowl marking the spot in the wall where Brian's head was?

I run my fingers through my dark tangle of hair and give myself a stern look in the chipped-edged mirror.

"Come on, Shaunna – be brave," I mutter. "Go and see what's happened."

Like a prizefighter (only I don't know many prizefighters who wear jeans and hippy cheesecloth tops), I take several short, sharp breaths to prime myself, before I step out into the ring. Or more accurately, the Singing Kettle café.

"Pssst!"

Sounds more like a hissing kettle than a singing kettle, but the *psssst* noise actually comes from Adam, who reaches over and hauls me down on to the chair next to him, right outside the ladies' loo.

"How's it going?" I whisper, not being able to see into the booth from here.

"Good," Adam whispers back, then takes a noisy suck on the straw in the Coke in front of him. "Check that out. . ."

His slurping is making me wince slightly, but I look in the direction he's pointing in. It's the old couple who run the place; they're leaning against each other, a checkered tea towel over each shoulder, staring dewy-eyed and fond in the direction of the booth I left my sister sitting in. I suddenly feel like I'm in a Disney movie – but maybe that's because Elton John's warbling *The Circle of Life* from *The Lion King* in the background, on the radio that Mr and Mrs Singing Kettle have got tuned to Radio Slush or whatever.

I can't resist – I've got to see what's stirred the romantic warm glow in Mr and Mrs Singing Kettle. In slow motion, I lean as far left as I can go without falling off my seat, and manage to sneak a sideways peek into the booth – where Ruth and Brian are holding hands and kissing across the table.

Awww. . .

"How did you get Bor – er, Brian to come here tonight?" I ask Adam brusquely, hoping my eyes aren't too give-away moist.

Adam told me on the phone last night that he was going to have to use an excuse, same as I was; after nearly a week of knockbacks from my sister, Boring Brian's confidence was so shattered that he didn't think he'd ever stand a chance of making any headway with Ruth.

"I just told him I needed to talk to him," says Adam matter-of-factly, slurping away at his ice-filled glass of Coke again. Not that I should let anything that petty wind me up; not when Adam has surpassed my expectations and managed to wangle this reunion so well.

"Yeah, but what did you say you wanted to talk to him about?" I ask, thinking of my own, fake, pining-after-Dean heart-to-heart.

Adam shrugs, batting his brown lashes over his green eyes as he seems to struggle to remember such an inconsequential detail.

"I told him I thought our parents were going to split up," he says casually.

"*What?!*" I squeak. "Adam – that's a *terrible* thing to say! How could you come up with something like that?!"

"Well, I needed a pretty strong excuse to get Brian to

come and talk to me alone, didn't I?" Adam explains himself blithely, while I shudder.

"But you must have really worried him!" I point out.

"Not as much as if I said one of them had cancer – and that was my first idea."

I'm so stunned, that although I want to punch Adam Pindar really hard for being so horrible, I'm rooted to the spot – open-mouthed – in shock.

"Course, I could have kept our mum and dad out of it, if I'd gone for my *other* idea," he announces.

"Which *was*?" I ask, knowing I'll probably regret it.

How right I am. . .

"I was going to tell Brian that I'd got a sexually transmitted disease, and could he tell me how to get rid of it."

I know Adam's only joking – because I can see the wicked grin on his face before I slap my hands across my eyes – but honestly, if anyone can ruin a moving, Hollywood-style reconciliation like the one going on three booths down, Adam can.

And if there's an award out there for Most Tactless, Gross, Disgusting Teenage Boy, he'd win, hands down. *No* problem. . .

chapter eleven

Something old, something naff...

Date: *Saturday 12th October*

State of mind: *Dutiful*

Sightings of Star-Boy: *In my dreams...*

I had a dream about Star-Boy last night. It was fantastic – it felt so real it almost made up for the fact that I haven't had any real-life sightings of him for *months*. (What if he's left town? Or what if he's left the country? Or what if he's dead? OK, enough of the depressing "what ifs"...)

What was *less* fantastic about my dream was that Adam Sodding Pindar was in it too – but only for a moment, and I think my subconscious chucked him in there just to illustrate the difference between oiks (and Adam's a perfect specimen) and love-gods (Star-Boy, natch).

Anyhow, the dream went like this: I'm walking along a rainy street, when a lad in a hooded jacket blocks my way, coming from the opposite direction. I try and move to get past, but he moves with me; so I try moving the other way, but he does too. This keeps on happening and I'm starting to get agitated, but the lad just starts laughing, like this is all one big joke to him. It's when I hear that laugh that I realize it's Adam; but in that split-second, a black cab screeches to a stop beside me, and the door is thrown open by Star-Boy, who grins that killer grin at me and motions for me to jump in. "Close your eyes and lean back," he tells me in this velvety voice, and I sink gratefully into the leather seat. Then he tells me to open my eyes, and I find myself leaning back in a boat now, staring up at a billowing white sail that contrasts sharply with the dark, night sky. The boat, I somehow know, is a felucca – which means we must be drifting along the Nile. (Isn't it brilliant that dreams let you do that? Just switch times, places and continuity?) The only sounds I can hear are the water buffalo gently lowing on the unseen, distant banks, water gently splashing on the sides of the little wooden boat, and – of course – Star-Boy's velvety voice, as he begins pointing out the constellations in the night sky above us. . .

"Yeeeooow!"

One second, I'm standing in the conservatory with Molly and Jude, just about to tell them all about my dream; the next, a sharp pain in the back of my legs has sent me hurtling towards the ground, cracking my knees sharply on the tiled floor.

"Haaaaaaaa-haaaaaaaa-haaaaaaaa!" shrieks an excitable small person, who's pointing at her crumpled handiwork (me) with great satisfaction.

"Oh, hello, Shaunna!" comes Mary Pindar's voice at the door that adjoins the living room. "Sorry about that – we keep hoping our Bethany will grow out of that bad habit!"

Maybe Mrs Pindar's monstrous grandchild would stop kicking people in the legs if someone gave her a kick back, I think grumpily, trying to blank out the pain I'm in and letting Molly and Jude help me get back on to my feet.

"It's OK," I lie, for the sake of good manners. "I didn't use my kneecaps much anyway."

Molly and Jude laugh, but Mrs Pindar only frowns in confusion. Oops, I forgot the Pindars are all a humour-free zone – apart from Adam, of course, but the less said about his juvenile sense of humour the better.

"Only joking," I explain. "Mrs Pindar, these are my friends, Molly and Jude; Molly, Jude, this is Bor – Brian's mum, and his niece, who's going to be Ruth's flowergirl."

"Ah!" mumbles Jude, trying to act polite, although I can tell she's on the verge of sniggering, after hearing all my stories about Bethany the mini Beelzebub. I can't even *look* at Molly; I can feel her shoulders shaking right next to me.

"So!" I start chatting conversationally, to cover up for my friends' giggles. "You've all got here all right, then?"

Our house is crammed with people right now: the entire McKay clan (Mum's side of the family) are here, along with loads of Granny's buddies, and – since the wedding is most definitely back on – Boring Brian's lot got an invite too. Thank God Mum let me ask Molly and Jude along to keep me company (and sane).

"Yes, we got here no problem. We took Lynsey, Bethany and the baby in our car, and Brian should be right behind us with Adam," trills Mrs Pindar, scooping up a wriggling Bethany.

"Great," I smile.

Urgh, I say silently to myself.

Adam must be what – sixteen now, same as me? You'd think he'd have better things to do than trail along to some corny party with his mum and dad, wouldn't you? I mean, much as I'd like to get out of it, it's not as if I *can*, seeing as it's my granny's do. My gran's golden wedding anniversary, to be precise. Which is pretty weird really, when you consider that her husband, my grandad, died long before I was even born. But then, that's my gran for you – as I said before, she's feisty and strong-willed, and when she told Mum and Dad she wanted to celebrate her anniversary, the only thing they could do was offer to have a party at ours, in exchange for her promising not to try and install her new electric shower herself, like she was threatening to do. (Which would probably have been the quickest way to reunite her with Grandad. . .)

"So which one is your grandmother, dear?" asks Mrs Pindar, struggling to hold on to her armful of kicking, spitting child. "Can you introduce me?"

Oh, please don't make me go back in there, I sigh silently, as I gaze into the packed, noisy living room. I only came out of there five minutes ago with my mates to escape the relentless comments I was getting from assorted relatives. I mean, how many times can you take someone saying, "Ooh, this is never Shaunna, is it? My, haven't you grown?!" Well, I'd be a concern to the medical profession if I hadn't. And then there's that other favourite: "What about your Ruth getting married, eh, Shaunna? *You'll* be next!" Not if I can help it. . .

"Sure, I'll introduce you," I try to say brightly, leading the way through to the other room. "Granny would love to meet you – she adores Brian."

But uh-oh, through the chattering throng, I can see Granny sitting on the sofa on the far side of the room, flanked by two friends from her sheltered housing block, and it doesn't look like she's in the mood for friendly introductions. Maybe it's the fact that she's totally dressed in black. Or maybe it's just that she's got a face like thunder.

"Listen, why don't we go and get Bethany some juice first?" I suggest instead, aiming Mrs Pindar and the gently screaming Bethany towards the kitchen instead. "Mol, Jude – can you sort them out? I'll be back in a minute. . ."

The girls both give me a quizzical look, but nod. Which leaves me free to go and find out what's going on. And I know something is, I can sense it. Peering around the sea of faces, I suddenly spot Dad out in the hallway chatting to my Uncle Eric, and make a beeline for him.

"Dad!" I hiss, giving Brian and Adam a cursory wave as I see them come through the front door. "What's happened?"

"Oh, I dunno – you better ask your mother," he sighs, knitting his hairy eyebrows together. "She's upstairs, with your sister."

Uh-oh – a confab upstairs while there's guests a-plenty milling about downstairs. It must mean trouble. . .

It's taken me twenty minutes to calm my mum and my sister down, but they're both a lot better now. At least they've stopped crying, and Mum's even attempting to repair her make-up before we make an entrance back downstairs.

So what happened? Quite a lot, it seems, while I was otherwise engaged being patronized by well-meaning aunties and uncles.

The first trauma was to do with Mum and my grandma. Mum got her knickers (justifiably) in a twist when, after *weeks* worth of planning, *days* worth of baking and *hours* worth of decorating the place, Granny turned up (in her all-black get-up) and suddenly announced she was going into a belated secondary phase of mourning. Now while I can't blame Granny for getting a touch sentimental about my dear, departed Grandad on the occasion of their anniversary, I can see that she's also a stubborn old moo who will refuse all coaxing and reasoning when she's in that kind of a mood. Poor Mum tried manfully to jolly Granny out of her self-induced misery – for the sake of everyone who'd turned up to celebrate – but there was no budging her from her gloomy Queen Victoria act. And that's when my tired and tearful mum decided that the whole do was a complete disaster and resorted to a sniffle in the privacy of her room.

Except she was joined a few minutes later by my sister, who'd managed to deeply offend Granny without meaning to, and inadvertently brought about Trauma No. 2.

"But you're right, Shaunna," says Ruth now, hugging the ugly onyx brooch to her chest. "I'll talk to Granny and say just what you said. . ."

Phew – solved that one. Here's the deal: Queen

Victoria – sorry, Granny – hauls Ruth to one side downstairs, and tells her that she wants to give her something "old" for her wedding, as part of that whole "Something old, something new, something borrowed, something blue" tradition. Ruth, being Ruth, is deeply touched, and waits expectantly while Granny rumbles about in her huge patent leather handbag (black, of course). Then out comes this hideous brooch; a great big thing that's supposed to be a pretty carving of a posy of flowers, but in that depressing black onyx looks like something that would be stuck on the front of a Victorian tombstone. Ruth, not being much of an actress (unlike me, after my sterling work getting her and Brian back together), is a tad slow with her grateful smiles (mainly 'cause she's trying hard not to grimace). Sadly for Ruth, this chunky monstrosity has huge sentimental value for Granny – it was a gift from Grandad (who was obviously a nice guy, but a nice guy with no taste). So Granny goes in a massive huff at Ruth's lack of gratitude, and retreats even more into Queen Victoria icy stateliness, while Ruth gets totally upset, running up here to Mum and they end up upsetting each other even *more* into the bargain.

Cue my arrival, with me throwing a few soothing "never mind her – everyone's having a lovely time!" words of comfort to my mum, and then coming up with my fantastic idea to appease Granny, while solving Ruth's dilemma about how to wear her "something old" gloomy chunk of stone without totally ruining the look of her wedding dress.

"Tell Granny that it means *so* much, you'll wear it pinned on the *inside* of your dress on the day, right next to your heart," I'd suggested, after turning the brooch round and round in my hands and trying to find some attractive angle to it (impossible).

Thankfully, Mum and Ruth were appeased. And now, they were just about ready to face everyone – including my morbid granny – again.

"Come on!" I say brightly, pulling open the bedroom door.

Mum and Ruth have got up, brushed themselves down, and are walking towards me, when we all freeze, and stare in confusion at each other.

"Isn't that Elvis?" asks Mum, turning her head slightly to listen closer to the music that's suddenly blasting out from downstairs.

"Yeah – it's *Jailhouse Rock*," I mutter, as I lead the way down the stairs.

"Shaunna! Quick!" says Molly, standing at the foot of the stairs and motioning me to hurry down. "You've got to see this!"

I take the stairs two at a time, followed by Ruth and Mum. Hanging on to the banister, the three of us peer into the living room, where we can hear not only the sound of Elvis, but clapping and whooping, too.

Good grief.

"Is that *Granny*?!" says Ruth dubiously, as we all stare at Adam jiving with The Black Widow in the middle of the room, surrounded by an encouraging throng.

"Is that my *mother*?!" asks Mum, as my giggling, flush-faced grandmother gets spun under Adam's arm.

Now, *there's* a vision I won't forget in a hurry. In fact I'll probably have nightmares about it tonight, which means

Adam Pindar will have infringed on my dreams for a second night running....

chapter twelve

Beauty is in the eye of the beholder (or not...)

Date: Saturday 9th November

State of mind: Resigned to my fate

Sightings of Star-Boy: One. But talk about timing...

"Shaunna, it's *my* treat," Ruth smiles appealingly at me.

It's nearly teatime on Saturday, and me and my sister have just spent the afternoon having yet another fitting for the meringues at Bella Bella (the wedding's three months away and counting), and right now, I just want to get to Jude's where we're having a girls' night in with pizza and a video. Bliss.

"But you don't *have* to treat me," I try to insist, as Ruth and the woman in the white coat manhandle me on to a high stool.

But I know it's a lost cause. I'm going to have to give in gracefully.

"Now my name's Kerry, and I just want you to relax and enjoy this – all right, Shaunna?" says the beauty counter girl, spreading out an alarming array of rainbow-coloured eyeshadows, plus an frightening looking metal object that I wouldn't be surprised to find out is used by gynaecologists.

What kind of makeover is this?

"It's an eyelash curler," explains Kerry, wasting no time and lunging at my eyes with the contraption.

"Anyway, think of this as a little try-out for your bridesmaid make-up. And think of it as a thank-you," I hear Ruth smile. (You can always hear Ruth smile when she talks, even above the piped-in musak and general hubbub of passing customers milling around us in the department store.)

"A thank-you for what?" I ask, as I feel Kerry clench and wrench my eyelashes.

"For everything! For getting me and Brian back together; for being my bridesmaid; for just being my sister. . ."

I gulp, and hope that Kerry doesn't tell me off for the trace of watery-ness trying to squeeze its way out of my left eye. Maybe it'll rust the eyelash curler.

"But you and Brian getting back together – that was two months ago!" I try to protest, ignoring the other soppy stuff Ruth's just said ('cause I'm too embarrassed and in danger of openly blubbing in full view of the general public).

"Yeah, I know – but I feel like I never told you how grateful I am," says Ruth. "I mean, it's better than ever between me and Brian now."

"Good," I murmur, my eyes now open, as Kerry begins smothering my face in gloop – must be foundation, which I never, ever use.

I notice that two middle-aged ladies have stopped to examine what's happening to me, and from the way they're frowning, I don't think they like what they see.

"Well, it was you *and* Adam," Ruth spoils the moment by adding HIS name. "I mean, Adam is such a sweetheart, isn't he?"

Oh, yes, Adam Pindar is such a sweetie. Everyone loves Adam – not just for getting the wedding back on course, but for jollying my grandmother along at her party last month and transforming her from the Scottish Widow to the Merry Widow, with the aid of a *Best of Elvis* album, a lot of flattery and a few underarm spins. It wasn't too much of a surprise that my gullible family fell for him after that, but I have to say that it was slightly galling to find out that Molly and Jude had fallen under his spell too.

"He's mad!" Jude giggled, when I slouched over to hers for a post-mortem the day after the party. "He's so funny!"

Well, that was easy for *her* to say. *She* wasn't the one who'd been dragged up in front of all her relatives to sing a karaoke version of *You're The One That I Want* later in the evening. When Adam yelled across the living room for me to join him, I wanted to run a hundred miles, but with a room full of baying relatives, I felt I had no choice, and ended up very, *very* reluctantly doing a terrible impression of Sandy from *Grease*, while Adam (as Danny, God help him) danced his way enthusiastically all around me.

Everyone loved it, except me. I think I'll carry the emotional scars for years. . .

"Anyway, remember Wayne?" Ruth continues, ignoring the fact that I've said nothing in reply to her statement about Adam being a sweetheart. (As if...)

"Brian's best man?" I reply, as Kerry fluffs and flutters around my face with a variety of implements.

"Yeah, well, you'll never guess – he's going to get us a widescreen TV with surround-sound for our wedding present!" Ruth gushes enthusiastically. "Isn't that brilliant?"

"Definitely," I mumble, as Kerry grips my chin firmly and starts painting some more gloop on to my lips.

Wow – Mr Moustache (Wayne) might have seemed pretty dull the one time I met him, but at least he seems to be generous. Although how a bloke who's a salesman at an electrical goods warehouse – same as Boring Brian – can afford such a big present, I'll never know. Maybe he's got a rich daddy. Maybe Wayne is the secret lovechild of Richard Branson...

"Mmm, Brian was saying we're going to have to start looking for a flat soon. We can't have all these presents and nowhere to put them. But I just said to him, Brian, let's not rush it; there'll be more properties to choose from if we wait till after the new year, and *he* said..."

I've tuned out; I'm aware of Ruth's voice babbling away, just as I'm aware of Kerry daubing at me and the two housewives looking on dubiously. But the reason I've tuned out is that I can hear a noise that somehow strangely reminds me of something familiar from a long time ago... I wrack my brains, zapping through my memory banks, then I stop, at the section in my mind labelled "Spooky".

And suddenly I know, sure as sure, like some mad old psychic, that in amongst the bunch of boys I hear laughing (the same laughter I heard one night long ago in Westburn Park) is a face I know nearly as well as my own. I may not have seen it for four months, but I fall asleep dreaming about that face every night. . .

"Whoa! You nearly made me smudge your lips!" says Kerry in alarm, as I sit bolt upright.

And there he is – Star-Boy, passing by me in slow-motion with his posse of mates, grinning that grin at *me*. God – *am* I psychic? How did he know to turn around and look at me? Was I sending out soul-mate vibes? Or could it be – could it be. . .

As the tall, beautiful lad that is Star-Boy turns away and slips through the revolving doors with his friends, the sparkly glitter of magic blows away from my shoulders and reality hits me like a sledgehammer.

"Give me a mirror," I order Kerry, with a wobble in my voice.

Kerry, her own face so caked in a layer of make-up it looks like a thin latex mask, passes me a long-handled mirror.

"It looks great!" Ruth enthuses, but I trust the tell-tale expressions on the two middle-aged shoppers more than my sister right now.

"Ohhhh. . ." I gasp softly, as I see my reflection.

The transformation is stunning. Only a few minutes ago, I was a reasonably attractive sixteen-year-old girl. Now I look like a forty-year-old lapdancer from the '80s. Plum lipliner, pink lipstick, blue and green eyeshadow . . . all set off with a big, bushy hairdo courtesy of the broad, black hairband Kerry's used to keep the hair off my face.

Nice – if you are, like I say, a forty-year-old lapdancer from the '80s. A disaster – if you're me and the only time you see the boy of your dreams is when you look like a *freak*.

Can my life get any more unfair?

"Oh, dear," mutters Kerry, reaching for a tissue and a bottle of cleanser. "You might be a bit allergic to that foundation – you're coming out in a terrible red rash."

I hear the two housewives tut, and see them cross their arms and study me hard, with all the fascination of being in at the scene of a car crash. . .

chapter thirteen

Christmas time, mistletoe and whine...

Date: *Wednesday 25th December*

State of mind: *Fuzzily festive*

Sightings of Star-Boy: *No boy-shaped presents under the tree, unfortunately*

Christmas is great when you're a kid; you get up at the crack of five, shriek yourself hoarse with excitement opening all your presents (and anyone else's you can get your hands on), and are genuinely thrilled at the small, useless plastic objects that fall out of Christmas crackers.

But when you get to my age, Christmas seems to be a little corny. Like those stupid paper hats that always slither off your head into your gravy, and the TV shows that are full of festive fun, even though you know they were recorded in September. And I wish my mum wouldn't spray that fake snow in our front windows – I'm sure all the neighbours snigger at it. I know *Granny* doesn't approve – "Isn't that white stuff terrible to clean off?" she asked Mum earlier, when she arrived for dinner. But she comes out with that every year – you can see her sitting in the armchair, frowning at it from a distance, and probably trying to work out whether a dollop of Cif Multi-Purpose Cleaner would shift it or if you'd need to resort to a blow-torch and a car windscreen scraper.

Anyway, after a dull day slouched in front of the telly watching a whole bunch of movies we've all seen tons of times before, our day is dull no more. That's not to say it's suddenly become *fun* or *interesting*; it's just not dull. The reason is, at my mother's invitation, zillions of Pindars have descended upon us: Boring Brian, his parents, Adam and Lynsey (complete with husband Barry and two sprogs).

Dad looks panicky; Mum has wandered off with the coats and Mrs Pindar, and left him to help Lynsey and Barry park their buggy in our hall. It's funny that he's driven all kinds of cars and vans over the years, but is now making a right meal of manoeuvring this small contraption. Course, it doesn't help that we have a demon child whirling around the confined space of the hallway, bouncing off walls like a pinball.

"Would you . . . um . . . would you like a chocolate, Bethany?" Dad tries to suggest, although his words are being drowned out by the ear-splitting whine of a fighter plane that's just about to crash. Oh, no – my mistake; it's Bethany.

"No, better not." Lynsey pulls a face at the mention of Dad's bribe. "It makes her hyperactive. . ."

Wow. If this is Bethany calm, then I'd hate to see her

after a couple of Cadbury's Creme Eggs. Our house would probably just end up a pile of rubble with a triumphant three-year-old standing in the middle of it.

"We thought she'd fall asleep in the car on the way over," drones Barry, who I've only seen in the distance before, at ickle Frankie's christening. "But she managed to stay awake somehow."

That's a miracle, I think as I grab Bethany in what hopefully looks like a hug, but is actually a restraining vice-like grip to give Dad a chance to sort out the buggy.

What I mean is, listening to a flat, toneless voice like Barry's, it's amazing Bethany didn't nod off, just like that. If he ever fancies a change from his AA day job, he could always retrain as a hypnotist. "When you hear me droning, you will start to feel *verrrryyy sleeeppppyyyy*. . ."

"ADAM!" Bethany yells sharply in my ear.

"OK! Let's go and find Adam!" I pretend to say cheerfully, picking up Bethany and carrying her through to the living room. "Will we see if Adam knows any good games to play?"

I was thinking of one called "Hide And Don't Seek". Bethany and Adam could go and hide – in the garden shed, say – and then I wander off and help myself to another dollop of trifle and do my best not to go and seek them.

"ADAM! ADAM! ADDDDAAAAAMMMM!"

I'm going to have tinnitus for life at this rate. Granny doesn't think much of this wailing banshee either – I can see by her face. I remember her once telling me about the old, Scottish tradition of giving a child a "skelp on the backside" when they were naughty, and from the way her hand is twitching right now, she seems to be sorely tempted to revive that ancient tradition, whatever child protection laws the government might come up with.

"Here – I'll take her!" says Ruth, appearing at my side and scooping her soon-to-be niece-in-law out of my arms.

"Thanks," I reply, unsure if I just yelled or whispered that, now I've been deafened.

"ADDDDAAAMMMM!" squeals Bethany, at a frighteningly high pitch. She practically scrambles up Ruth's chest and over her shoulder as ADDDDAAAMMMM! walks into the living room.

"Hello, Mrs McKay!" he sucks up to my granny, as he strides over to Ruth and the gremlin and slaps his hand lightly across Bethany's mouth. It sends her into fits of muffled giggles. I wouldn't have dared do that – that kid has some sharp-looking teeth, and I can't remember the last time I had a tetanus jab.

"There you go!" Ruth smiles, gratefully passing the Bethany-shaped parcel to her uncle. "Hey, Shaunna – why don't you take Adam up to your room and show him your CD collection? I was telling him how much of a music fan you were!"

Adam grins at me. I've never noticed how big his mouth is before; when he smiles, it looks like someone cut out a picture of a smile and then stuck it on a photo of a much smaller head. He's just one big grin, like the Cheshire Cat. Weird.

"Whatever," Adam shrugs, sounding less than thrilled with Ruth's suggestion, even though his face is still plastered with that inane, ear-to-ear grin.

Ruth, having come up with her lousy idea (I mean, like

I'd really want Adam Pindar, complete with Bethany, since she's limpeted herself to him, in my room?), now deserts us to go and drool over baby Frankie, who's asleep and dribbling in his mother's arms.

Adam is still staring at me – he expects me to say something, and I don't know what that should be. It certainly isn't, "Yeah! Come up and make jibes about my taste in music! And bring the human wrecking ball while you're at it!"

"So. . ." says Adam, ending the microsecond silence. "What about your super-slapper makeover last month?!"

My heart misses a beat or three. Oh, the *shame* – did he see me? Was he there at the department store that day?

"Whaaa?" I manage to squeak.

"Ruth told me about it. Said you hated it," he explains, as his head is tugged sharply sideways by the hair.

Phew.

Phew that no one else witnessed the true horror of the dreaded '80s makeover (as if Star-Boy wasn't bad enough). And phew to the fact that it wasn't me holding on to Bethany and having hunks of hair ripped out of my head.

"Well, it wasn't *great*," I mumble, trying to hold on to a shred of dignity by going into denial. "But it wasn't exactly *slapper*-ish."

"Ruth told me that was exactly what you said about it on the way home!" Adam insists, and annoyingly, he is right.

Riiiiiiiiinnnnnnnnnnnnngggggggggg!!!!!!

"Shaunna! Can you get that?" Mum's voice drifts through above the babble of voices going on in our house.

But before she'd even finished the sentence, I've darted off to answer the front door, glad of any excuse to get away from Adam and the troll-baby.

"Oh, Shaunna!" whimpers Jude, as soon as I haul open the door.

From the tears on her face, and the pack of cigarettes she's clutching, I can see that what my friend's got for Christmas is a trauma of some kind or another.

Nice one, Santa.

"How could he, Shaunna?" Jude snuffles.

It's very cold out here in the garden, despite the layers of coats and scarves I threw on both of us before I hustled Jude straight down the hall and out of the back door. We're now hiding behind the shed, so Jude can have her cigarette without shocking my mother, and Jude has just spilt out her festive woes to me.

What happened was that Helen (being Helen) made plans to meet up with friends tonight, which might seem a little lacking in it's-a-time-for-families sentiment on this day of all days. (Oh, yes; however corny I think Christmas is, I still kind of *like* sitting round the table with my folks and groaning at the terrible jokes in the crackers.) Anyway, Jude wasn't too surprised or disappointed – she thought it would be great to have the house to herself and invite Scott round for a romantic night in. So, Scott turns up, but instead of mistletoe and snogging, Jude ends up being informed that she's chucked, because Scott – poor lamb – is bored.

"I mean, it hasn't been great *all* the time between us," Jude snuffles on, "but it wouldn't be normal to be great all the time, would it?"

"Yeah, but it comes down to percentages, doesn't it?" I reason with her.

Jude frowns. Her mind always switches to a state of confusion when it comes to maths.

"What I mean is, you have to think; how much of the time would you say you were happy when you were with him, and how much of the time *wasn't* so good?"

Jude is silent, scrunching up her forehead in concentration.

"You don't have to work it out *exactly*," I tell her. "It's just that you've got to be happy with someone about seventy to eighty per cent of the time, or it's just not worth it. Get it?"

Jude nods.

"And *were* you happy about seventy to eighty per cent of the time you were with Scott? *Honestly?*"

After a pause, Jude shakes her head.

"Well, there you go, then. You've just got to—"

"Is someone *smoking* out here?!" booms a deeply masculine voice.

Jude jumps into automatic pilot mode, dropping her cigarette and stamping on it, while frantically flapping the smoke away with both her hands.

She needn't have bothered – a grin attached to a head appears around the side of the shed, and Adam sniggers out loud at his latest "gotcha!".

"Wassup?" he asks, looking from me, to Jude and back again.

"Go away, Adam – we're having a private talk," I tell him.

"Jude?! Are you *crying*?" he asks my friend, like he hasn't even heard me speak.

"She's OK; just leave us—"

"Adam – I got chucked!" Jude blurts out.

"Nah!" says Adam, in what's probably mock surprise. He's going to make a joke out of this, I know he is. It's not the right time, but it's just the sort of insensitive thing he'd do, and if he does, then I'm going to have to kill him.

"Yeah!" sobs Jude. "Said he was bored of going out with me!"

"Bored of going out with *you*? Are you *kidding*?!" gasps Adam, coming ever closer to getting a "skelp" from me, if he puts a foot wrong. "This bloke's *got* to be brain-dead! That's the only explanation!"

Jude blinks her watery eyes at him in confusion.

"Is he brain-dead, Jude?"

Jude shakes her head.

"Are you sure? Did you check?"

OK – enough. I'm going to have to wade in here and kill him.

"Or he could be *dead*-dead! That's the only way someone could be bored being with a gorgeous girl like you!"

I'm just about to open my mouth and tell Adam Pindar that the only person around here who's going to be dead is him, when I hear a strange noise.

It's Jude. And she's giggling.

"You know what you need, don't you?" Adam ploughs on.

"No – what?" smiles Jude.

"Revenge!" Adam growls theatrically. "You want to get

out and snog *loads* of really cool guys and make this loser pig-sick!"

"Cool guys like who?" asks Jude, looking momentarily sad – she's obviously still working under the misapprehension that Scott is a cool guy.

"Like . . . me!" grins Adam, throwing his arms out. "I'd be happy to help you out by letting you snog me!"

"Adam!" I glare at him.

"No – it's not a problem; I don't mind at all. It's all in a good cause!"

Adam steps towards Jude, lunging his puckered lips at her. I'm pretty sure he's just fooling around, and Jules is giggling like crazy, but just to be on the safe side, I shove my arm out and block his way.

For a split-second, Adam gives me a strange little glance, as if he thinks I'm being a spoilsport or something. But whatever, he seems to calm down.

"Anyway, maybe you'll meet someone at my brother's wedding," he says to Jude. "There's always loads of talent at weddings."

Talent? What a naff word. And why was he saying that to Jude? Numbers were pretty tight, the invitations had gone out, and Jude certainly wasn't on the list, much as I'd have loved her to be. And that was kind of unfair, since Molly would be going, as Dean's guest, of course.

"But I haven't been invited to the wedding!" Jude protests.

"Yes, you have! To the reception, anyway," Adam contradicts her.

"Who says?" I frown at him. I'm always frowning at Adam Pindar. Which is why I don't like being around him too much. If I end up needing Botox injections to cure premature frown lines, then I'm sending the bill to him. . .

"Your sister just said," he replies, nodding his head backwards towards the house. "'Cause Brian was saying that it's OK for me to take a couple of my mates to the reception, so Ruth said in that case it was only fair that you got to invite Jude."

It's good news – I just wish I wasn't hearing it from this particular, grinning source.

"So . . . are you two going to stay out here and get frostbite?" asks Adam. "Or are you going to come in and get a glass of that Bailey's my dad's pouring out for everyone?"

Adam holds a gentlemanly arm out for us both, and while Jude wraps her arm around his, I pretend I haven't noticed and pad up the path ahead of them.

"Course, if you don't fancy snogging me," I hear Adam say to Jude, "there are a lot of cool guys you could start on inside. I mean, there's *my* dad, or *Shaunna's* dad . . . *fwoargghhh*, eh?"

That's Jude off in giggles again, which is a good thing, I suppose.

And there has been one other good thing today, actually. Just like every year since I can remember, me and Ruth got to split the wishbone, and this year, for the first time ever that I can remember, I got the bigger half. And what was my Christmas wish? That after nearly a year of dreaming and glimpses, I'm going to finally come face-to-close-up-face with Star-Boy.

It might make it difficult to do homework or wash my hair or whatever, but until that moment comes, I think I'll

129

keep my fingers crossed on both hands – well, there's no harm in giving my wish a helping hand, is there?

chapter fourteen

Hen night hell

Date: *Saturday 8th February*

State of mind: *Aghast*

Sightings of Star-Boy: *So close ... and yet so far*

I can't quite believe what's happening. I – Shaunna Sullivan, aged sixteen and a quarter – am sitting in a horseshoe-shaped booth in the scuzziest, tackiest nightclub in town (strictly over-21s only), with a large, lardy, sweaty bloke gyrating centimetres from my face.

Actually, it's worse than that. The lardy bloke is wearing nothing but a pair of cowboy boots and a teeny, tiny, red, wet-look G-string (unless you count the fact that he's got so much body hair he looks like he's got a brown fuzzy jumper on). And the thing is, the lardy bloke isn't just standing in front of me; oh no. He is leaning (and leering) over me, giving me what I think is supposed to be a lap-dance.

I hope he doesn't expect me to put any money down his G-string. And I hope this table's reinforced – there's a lot of heavy-duty lard undulating about up there, and I don't want it collapsing on top of me.

"Over here! Over *here*! *This* one's the bride!"

Oh, good – Ruth's two best mates Justine and Penny have grabbed the lardy bloke (one by the arm and one by the G-string) and hauled him over to their side of the table, so he can do his unsexy thing for Ruth. Who is at this moment sitting in between Justine and Penny with her hands slapped over her face. Not that you can see much of her head anyway, since Justine and Penny have gaffer-taped a white sheet around her head as a looky-likey veil.

Then just when I think it's safe, the lardy bloke turns, gives me a wink and says, "Meet me for a drink later, babes?"

I shake my head so hard I give my neck whiplash, while the girls I'm surrounded by – college buddies of Ruth's – cackle so much they nearly spill their pint glasses of cocktails.

Welcome to hell.

And somewhere across town, is heaven. Or at least a really brilliant-sounding party, which I could have been at with Jude and Molly, if I hadn't had to come along to my sister's hen night. I tried to get out of it, I really did. I pulled the excuse that I was *well* under age to get into Romeo's (chosen, by the way, for its general cheesiness and male strippers), but Ruth just told me they'd put me in the middle of a huddle of her girlfriends, and no one on the door would stop me. I really, really hoped the doorman was both eagle-eyed and diligent about his job, but it didn't work out that way; the guy in the black suit just chewed on his gum, stared into space, and waved us all in. We could have been a party of nine-year-old Brownies for all he cared.

Apart from the fact that Romeo's just isn't my kind of place (put it this way, in all the years it's been open, I don't think a Nirvana track has ever sullied its decks), I knew when she asked me that I'd just stick out like a sore thumb amongst Ruth's crowd of mates. I mean, I don't know any of the girls from college, and her old schoolfriends Justine and Penny have always been about as interested in me as they are in watching championship golf on the telly (ie not a lot). And it's turned out as bad as I thought; everyone except me is drunk as a skunk (I've been sipping on the same cocktail since I arrived – it's so disgustingly sweet it's like swallowing condensed milk), and screaming and cackling together like a bunch of hyperactive witches. I know they're having fun, but I just wish I was somewhere else right now, cackling like a hyperactive witch with my *own* friends. . .

"Wanna 'nother drink?" the girl right beside me bellows in my ear. I think her name is Louise, but I'm not sure. Ruth's been too busy being hijacked by Justine and Penny to introduce me, so I've just tried to listen in to the girls talking to each other and pick up their names. I did attempt to say hello and tell them my name when we first sat down, but I got as far as "I'm Ruth's sister, Shau—" when they all nodded at me and started talking over the top of my head.

"No, it's OK – I've still got this drink to finish," I say to the girl-who's-maybe-Louise.

"Ah, go on!" she slurs at me.

"No, honestly," I shake my head.

"Ciggie?"

"No. No thanks."

I can tell by the way this girl is looking at me that she thinks I'm a freak. But I can't help it if I don't want to smoke or, drink coconut-flavoured condensed milk, find the stripper creepy rather than funny, and am the only girl around our table not wearing a boob tube.

"You know something?" says the girl-who's-maybe-Louise, as she struggles to find the end of her cigarette with her lighter.

"What?"

"You've caused a bit of hassle, you have."

"Me?" I frown. What could I have done?

"Justine and Penny," says the girl, pointing over vaguely in their direction. "They are *seriously* not chuffed that you're a bridesmaid, and they're not. . ."

Great. I was wondering what the particularly frosty faces were for this evening. I could feel the cold shoulders they were giving me even on this side of the table. But how rubbish is that? Ruth picked me, purely because she couldn't choose between her two best mates, and then they end up resenting *me*, and not her.

This sucks. I need a break for a minute.

"'Scuse me – just going to the loo," I smile at the girl-who's-maybe-Louise, then shuffle past her and another few pairs of knees, all the while trying to avert my eyes from the huge spotty bottom swaying about on the table.

Squeezing through the dancefloor (packed with girls

baying at the lardy bloke), I fumble my way into the quiet calm of the ladies' loos, and lock myself away in the nearest cubicle.

God, I feel trapped. If I try and come up with an excuse and leave now, Ruth will be really hurt; but if I stay, I think my head will explode from the effort of fake-smiling. Oh, and tomorrow's going to be nearly as bad. Mum – at Granny's instigation – has revived another old Scottish tradition; something called the Show of Presents (which sounds more like it should just be called "Showing Off" to me). It involves setting out all the wedding gifts that Ruth and Brian have been sent, so that our living room looks like a display area in the home section of BhS. Then hordes of friends, family and neighbours (all female, by the sounds of it), come and ooh and aah at the pressies, and expect cake and tea in payment for their compliments. The whole idea is totally bizarre, and if I had my way (when do I *ever* when it comes to this wedding), I'd spend the day hiding out over at Jude's. But that's not going to happen, because Mum has demanded that the bridesmaid-to-be (me) is there to meet, greet and serve nibbly bits to our guests.

Give me strength. . .

The muffled sounds of *Teenage Dirtbag* shake me out of my misery, and I fumble madly in my bag for my mobile.

"Hello?"

"Shaunna?" says Molly's voice, although it's hard to make out her voice above the pounding music in the background.

"Mol?" I smile, grateful to hear a familiar, friendly voice. "How's the party?"

"Great!" she yells down the phone. "But listen – got

stuff to tell you. Hold on, I'll try and go somewhere quieter."

There's some muffles and shuffles, and something that sounds like a door closing, and the music sounds further away.

"OK, that's better," says Molly. "Can you hear me better?"

"Yeah – definitely. Where are you?"

"The coat cupboard under the stairs. Honestly, this place is mobbed!"

"Uh-huh, but what stuff have you got to tell me?" I hurry her along, curiosity getting the better of me.

"Well, I've got some good news. Oh, no – maybe it's bad. And I've got some *definitely* bad news. Which do you want first?"

"Well, between a choice of bad news and definitely bad news, I guess I'll start with the *definitely* bad news."

Urgh – it's safe to say that any curiosity has now been replaced by *dread*.

"Well, the *definitely* bad news is that it looks like Jude's back together with Scott."

"What?!" I squeal. After all the weeks of comforting her and talking her out of still fancying that creep. . .

"Yeah – he turned up at the party, and me and Dean just walked in on them snogging in the kitchen."

Now I was glad I wasn't there. I'd be too disappointed to see Jude mess up again first-hand. It was bad enough hearing about it over the phone.

"And there's someone else at the party too," Jude continues. "That's my good news/bad news thing. It's him. Star-Boy."

I am in hell. I'm in a loo that's decorated with bad murals of naked Greek gods that are so naff it makes you want to grab a pen and graffiti some underwear on them, and meanwhile, Star-Boy is wandering about at a party I should have been at.

"Is he alone?" I ask, my heart thunk-thunking.

"He's with –"

Oh, no . . . she's cutting out.

"– mates. He's not with . . . hello? Can you—"

Damn – she's gone. Useless mobile phones. . .

I'm just about to dial her number and reconnect with the coat cupboard at the party, when my phone rings first.

"Molly?" I gasp. "God, I'm so gutted. I can't believe he's there and I'm not!"

"What?" says a voice that doesn't belong to Molly. Or a girl, for that matter.

"What?" I say back, confusion sending my cheeks hot pink, I can tell.

"Shaunna?"

"Yes – who's this?"

"Adam," says Adam.

Perfect. I'm sitting on the toilet with my trousers round my ankles, my heart crushing nicely, and feeling like a fool. It's totally fitting that my misery is added to with a call from Adam Pindar.

"Adam – why are you phoning me?" I demand, standing up hurriedly and trying to sort myself out. "Aren't you supposed to be at the stag party?"

"I am. I mean, I was," he bumbles.

Is he drunk? I wonder.

"Anyway, I didn't mean to phone you – I was trying to

call Ruth, but she must have her mobile switched off."

"Well, *yeah*. It is her hen party," I point out. "I don't suppose she's expecting too many calls tonight. Anyway, shouldn't you being tying Brian naked to a lamppost about now?"

Stag party pranks: that would be *right* up Adam's street.

"Whatever," says Adam, almost brusquely, which doesn't sound like him at all. "Look – you've got to get her. Something's happened."

"Something what?" I ask, frozen in alarm. Somehow I don't think this is going to end up in a dubiously funny punchline, the way Adam's stories generally do.

"I'm at Bell Street police station, Shaunna. Brian's been arrested."

I wait for half a second, just to be sure there definitely *isn't* a punchline to this; that it's not some let's-wind-up-the-hen-party joke. When Adam says nothing, apart from asking if I'm still there, I realize he's telling the awful truth.

"Shit," I fluster down the phone, as I fumble to unlock the cubicle door. "We'll be right there, Adam. . ."

In the living room, a pale-faced Ruth is dishing out tea and scones to Granny and a bunch of her handbag-clutching friends.

Apart from them, no one else has turned up yet to coo at the presents, so I've been excused for a bit, since Molly's turned up to fill me in with all the gossip from the party last night. But first, I've got to fill *her* in on all the gossip from the worst hen party of all time.

"He was *arrested*!" Molly is goggling wide-eyed at me, as

we hide out in the kitchen.

"Yeah, well, by the time me and Ruth got to the police station, they were releasing him," I explain.

If they hadn't already let Boring Brian go (with a caution) I think the desk sergeant would have relented anyway, after he was faced with a sobbing wreck of a fiancée, still wearing a sheet taped around her head and begging for mercy.

"So what exactly happened?" Molly grins, enjoying this as much as any episode of *The Bill*.

"Well, you know Boring Brian's mate Wayne? The one I told you is going to be the Best Man?"

Molly nods.

"What happened was, Wayne was up at the bar, getting a round of drinks for everyone," I carry on explaining, "when he gets jumped by these two blokes. Brian spots this, and dives in to rescue Wayne, and it all turns into the Wild West, with fists flying everywhere."

"But that's *so* unfair!" Molly cries. "Brian was just trying to help, and he gets arrested?"

"It's more complicated than that," I shrug. "It turns out that the two blokes who jumped on Wayne were undercover policemen."

Molly gasps. Which is what the whole stag party must have done when they found out.

"And they weren't trying to mug Wayne; they were trying to arrest him for paying for the drinks with a stolen credit card. . ."

"Ooh, that's terrible!"

"I know," I nod. I've been hearing about how terrible it is for half the night, since no one in our house went to bed till four am, after talking over every detail endlessly. It seems that Brian's Best Man could be up for a Best at Stealing Award; he had a wallet full of stolen cards and a house full of DVD players and microwaves, all nicked from work. No wonder he'd so generously offered to get Ruth and Brian a snoot TV as a wedding present – he wasn't going to be paying for it. . .

"Anyway, enough about my night," I waved away the horrible memories. "What about yours? Come on – tell me all about Jude and Scott."

"And. . .?" Molly grins at me, raising her blonde eyebrows skyward.

"And tell me all about Star-Boy," I grin back, my entire intestines spasming at the thought of him. (Might not sound very nice, but actually feels very pleasant indeed. . .)

"Well, I—"

"Hello, girls!" trills Granny, bustling into the kitchen with a tray of cups and flicking on the kettle. "Running out of tea through there, but with poor Ruth in the state she's in, I thought I'd come and do the needful. . ."

"She's all right, isn't she?" I ask, hoping she's not started crying again. It took me ages to do her make-up this morning so she looked half-alive after only half a night's sleep. She can't afford to cry any more – she's getting married on Friday, and needs to give her eyes a chance to calm down from their bloodshot state.

"She's holding up all right," Granny assures me (I'm sure she's loving all this drama), "but she's just a bit shell-shocked still, what with all the last-minute changes."

"What last-minute changes?" I frown. Last night was

just a blip; it hadn't changed anything to do with the wedding itself. Had it?

"The business of the Best Man, of course, Shaunna!" says Granny, swilling the cups under the tap. "Wayne can't exactly do the honours if he's in a prison cell, now can he?"

Doh. I hadn't thought about that. . .

"And Adam was happy to step in, but there's the alterations to the Best Man's suit to think of, and it'll be a terrible rush. . ."

"Wow! Adam's going to be Best Man!" Molly exclaims. "That'll be fun for you!"

"Will it?" I pull a face at her.

"Course it will!" says Adam's biggest fan (Granny), as she dries the teacups with a towel. "I'll be looking forward to seeing you two tripping around the floor together!"

"What do you mean?" I splutter. As far as I'm aware, Adam will stand on one side of Ruth and Brian when they take their vows, and I'll stand on the other. Then we'll both sign something or other as witnesses. And of course, we'll be sharing the top table at the reception with the bride and groom and parents. But apart from that, there's nothing else to be done. Including tripping around the floor, whatever Granny means by that.

"The wedding waltz, Shaunna, dear!" Granny says, slightly impatiently, as if I'm being super-dense. "You know – the bride and groom take to the floor to dance in front of everyone. . ."

I nod, vaguely aware that that's part of the whole wedding tradition.

". . .followed by the Best Man and the bridesmaid!"

It's funny, I've had all year to get used to the idea of this wedding, and it still hadn't sunk in properly till now. In five days' time, I will be expected to WALTZ (dear God!), with ADAM PINDAR (noooooo!), in a polyester MERINGUE (eeek!) in front of LOADS of people.

And unlike faking a tummy bug on the day of a particularly nasty maths test, there's not an excuse on earth that's going to get me out of *this* one. . .

chapter fifteen

Ready, steady, go!

Date:	*Friday 14th February (later)*
State of mind:	*Stuffed with butterflies migrating from my tummy*
Sightings of Star-Boy:	*Fat chance*

I know I'm jumpy, but Mum's hat is kind of scaring me.

Up close it's not so bad – it's a big, wide, puffy thing made of beige silk, with a darker brown silk on the underside of the brim. It's just that from a distance, it looks like a giant, mutant mushroom is eating my mother's head. Her face is pretty panicky, but I know that's got less to do with alien hats and more to do with the fact that Bethany is running around the house screaming that she won't wear her flowergirl outfit if she can't keep her wellies on.

Dad is flustering about, quietly getting an ulcer and repeitively playing with his cufflinks, while Granny is dealing with stress her own way – standing at the kitchen sink in her posh powder-blue suit and hat, matched with a pair of yellow Marigolds as she methodically takes clean glasses out of the cupboard and gives them a "freshen up" in soapy water. Mum's too frazzled trying to corral Bethany with Lynsey to tell Granny she's being ridiculous.

While the madness continues downstairs, I slope off up to my room – this is my one chance to try and repair the damage done by the hairdresser this morning. Jude and Molly were right all those months ago: I *did* have heated rollers inflicted upon me. And right now, staring at myself in my dressing table mirror, I have to admit that the scraped-up, piled-high style makes my head look like a coconut with a bad perm. My brown hair has been pulled up so tightly into a topknot that I've practically had a face-lift.

Slowly, I pull out the fake flowers that have been stuffed into the topknot (and into my head in places), yank the tight elastic band off and sigh in relief as the curls tumble down. They're still stupidly tight (and hairsprayed till crispy), but I reckon that if I turn my head upside down and comb through it with my fingers, I should be able to slacken it out so it's more wavy than curly. . .

"Shaunna?"

I turn and look at my upside-down sister in the doorway. Even this way up (or down) I can tell something isn't quite right. The cars are due here in five minutes, and Ruth is still wearing her dressing gown. And I thought *I* was rushing it, trying to dismantle my hairdo in such a short time.

"Are you OK?" I ask, straightening up too fast and going a bit wobbly.

"I just wanted to give you this. . ." says Ruth, a wonky little smile wavering on her face as she pulls a small box out of the pocket of the dressing gown.

"What is it?" I ask, taking the box from her.

"A present; for being my bridesmaid." She tries to smile, and fails miserably.

"Ruth?"

I'm staring at the weird expression on her face, trying to figure out what's going on. I'm still clutching the box, but checking out my present is the last thing on my mind when I've got one half-dressed, half-tearful looking sister standing in front of me.

"What's wrong, Roo?"

That's funny; I haven't called her Roo since I was about Bethany's age, and couldn't get my tongue around the "th" part of her name.

"I don't *know*!" my sister sighs, flopping down on the corner of my bed.

Her make-up's done, I notice, as is her hair, apart from the small rollers she's got bobbing about on either side of her face to give her ringlets. The way her dressing gown gapes open when she sits forward, I can see Granny's clunky black brooch pinned to her white basque, right above her heart.

"*What* don't you know, Roo?" I ask, sitting down beside her.

She *definitely* looks weird, my sister. But then Ruth always looks weird when she isn't smiling. It's just so unnatural not to see her like that.

"I . . . oh, I don't *know* what I don't know!" she shrugs helplessly in reply.

Uh-oh. Is this the famous Last Minute Nerves people are meant to get? The sort of thing that leaves jilted partners standing at the altar, mortified and humiliated in front of hundreds of guests? Oh, my God – is she having second thoughts about Boring Brian and their engaged/married/have 2.4 children/an estate car and a Tesco Club Card life plan?

"You . . . you haven't changed your mind, have you?" I ask tentatively, watching the clock on my bedside table and feeling a wave of panic wash over me. At this rate, we're going to be really late for the wedding – if there's going to be a wedding at all, of course. . .

"Changed my mind about Brian? No! I mean, I love him, but. . ."

"But?"

Ooh, I don't like the sound of that "but".

"But it's . . . well, it just what's going on today. It's all so complicated, this whole wedding thing," Ruth mumbles, twisting the belt of the dressing gown around in her hands. "It's like I've spent all year planning it and now it's so . . . so mind-blowingly *big* it's scary – not romantic, like I thought it would be!"

Tell me about it. Why's it taken her all this time to work that one out?

"Ruth, I thought you *loved* organizing all this!" I point out in surprise. "I thought you *loved* the fuss!"

"I guess I did . . . *do* . . . whatever," says Ruth, looking a little lost. "But *should* it have been more romantic? I mean, I can't help thinking maybe me and Brian should have run away, just the two of us, and got married on a tropical island or something. . ."

"Do you?" I ask her, wondering why she hadn't thought of this twelve months ago, instead of twenty minutes before she was due to be standing in front of the vicar and a church full of glammed-up friends and relatives.

"Hmm, yes, sometimes I do. But I don't think Brian would have liked that. Maybe . . . maybe that's the trouble. Maybe we're just not very romantic people. . ."

"Course you're romantic!" I tell her, grabbing hold of her cold, shaky, belt-twisting hands. "You two are the most romantic couple I know! You've been together since you were *twelve*, you know *all* each other's stories, but you *never* get bored with each other . . . that's so sweet! *That's* romantic!"

"Do you think so?" Ruth gives me the tiniest hint of a smile.

"Definitely!"

You know, when I blabbed that stuff right now, I wasn't just saying it to make Ruth feel better. I mean, I *was*, but as soon as the words came out of my mouth, I realized it was true: in their own way, Ruth and Boring Brian *are* pretty romantic.

"But loads of people seem to have more *passionate* relationships than us. We're just sort of . . . comfy!" Ruth flaps her hands around.

"Comfy can be romantic! There's lots of ways to be romantic!" I assure her. "And anyway, being happy is what matters. Sometimes, romantic stuff doesn't make you happy at all. . ."

I'm thinking, all of a sudden, about Star-Boy. For a

whole year to the day now, he's filled my head and my heart, no matter how I've tried to forget him (and OK, I haven't tried very hard to forget him). Unrequited love; that's something out of Russian novels, and Hollywood movies, and there's nothing more romantic than that. But is it making me happy? Actually, no. When Molly told me about seeing him at that party last week? Even though she said she didn't see him with another girl, that didn't console me, or stop the hurting, the aching, the *longing* that's been eating me up inside ever since. This whole crush on him; it's starting to be less of a warm, special secret and more of a sad, heart-crushing misery as time goes by, but I just don't know how I can stop myself being obsessed by him. . .

"Um . . . are you talking about something that's happened to *you*, Shaunna?" Ruth is looking at me warily.

I should tell her. Me and Ruth, we've never got into "sharing our feelings" (or spilling our guts), not like me with Jude and Molly, not like her with her mates Justine and Penny, but maybe it's time I gave it a try. Maybe Ruth'll have some amazing, sisterly insights that'll make sense of it all. Maybe—

"Ruth! What on *earth*. . .!" says Mum, standing in the doorway with her head-eating hat. "Come on! The car's going to be here in a second and you haven't even got your *dress* on!"

Ruth goes to stand up, following Mum's orders, then stops, glances down at me, and bends over to give me a quick, tight squeeze. She smells nice; she smells of delicate perfume and flowers and Ruth.

"Ruth!" Mum barks in a blind panic. "Come on!"

And so Ruth "comes on", scurrying out of my room and into her own.

Mum is on the verge of following, before she stops dead in the doorway and gazes at me askance.

"Shaunna, what *have* you done to your beautiful hair!"

I glance at myself in the mirror, and see a messy tangle of hippy-looking waves.

Hey, I'm a rock'n'roll bridesmaid!

Cool. . .

chapter sixteen

Do you, Ruth,
take Boring Brian...

Date: *Friday 14th February*

State of mind: *Covered in confetti*

Sightings of Star-Boy: *So wishes do come true...*

You know those floppy bunches of chemically-dyed chrysanthemums you can buy at petrol stations? Well, they're not the *only* kind of blue flowers around.

I know I once thought that, but Granny soon put me and Ruth straight, when we came back from that first fitting for my bridesmaid's dress last summer, and I was moaning on about being allergic to apricot. No sooner did the blue debate come up then Granny stopped Brasso-ing our letterbox, and immediately began counting off nature's blue wonders on her fingers: Cornflowers, Morning Glory, Forget-Me-Nots, Love-In-A-Mist, African Lily, Campanula, Cupid's Dart, Bellflower, Iris, Grape

Hyacinth . . . we had to physically restrain her before she got on to shrubs and wildflowers, and when Dad went to drive her home, she was still muttering on about going to look up flower encyclopaedias next time she was at the library.

But I'm very grateful for Granny's horticultural rant. Now Ruth's wedding day – Valentine's Day – has finally arrived, I may *still* have been forced into a layered meringue, but at least it's a *blue* layered meringue, to match the spring bouquet of bluebells, lily-of-the-valley and trailing ivy that Ruth is carrying. Me and Bethany, we've got tiny posies of snowdrops – they're very sweet.

And speaking of sweet (and I'm not being ironic here), Bethany is holding my hand and swaying gently, singing softly to herself, as we stand in front of the vicar – along with Ruth, Boring Brian, and Adam – while everyone bellows and warbles out "All Things Bright And Beautiful" behind us.

"*All things blah and blah-blah-blah. . .*" I hear Bethany's voice contentedly drift up.

This is all very surreal – being here in this imposing church; wearing fancy dress; Bethany behaving.

Actually, Bethany behaving isn't all that surreal or miraculous: I'm now officially her *bestest* friend in the world, and for good reason. In the chaos of trying to get Ruth ready, Mum enlisted Lynsey's help, and left me to deal with the drama of disengaging a wailing Bethany from her wellington boots.

At first I thought it was going to be a mission impossible, then I realized that it could all be resolved, with a little compromise and imagination. After all, that's what's worked for me; my mum may be disappointed that I demolished my lacquered curls and fake flower hairdo, but the loose girly waves and the snowdrop I pulled from my posy and pinned to one side of my head are still much more dressed up than I'd ever wear my hair normally.

So, when I found myself staring at a screeching, tomato-faced, wellie-wearing banshee, I was suddenly struck by inspiration. Five minutes later, a sparkly-eyed, placid Bethany was clambering into a posh black car beside me, a pair of angel wings (that I bought from TopShop and wore for a laugh to the school Christmas party) attached to the back of her white flowergirl frock, happily waving a glittery wand (ditto). She looked cute enough to eat, and even if Mum, Mrs Pindar and Lynsey all gave disapproving looks when me and Bethany trotted down the aisle, I could tell by all the "Awww!"s and smiles going on that everyone else thought she looked adorable.

And I don't think anyone's spotted her wellies yet – her dress is so long that only the tiniest hint of a rainbow-coloured rubber toe can be seen. . .

Right, that'll be the hymn finished, then. That was hymn number two: there was one earlier, with the vicar having a little chat about life, love and everything in between. I know it's terrible, but I haven't really been taking in what he's saying, my mind's so numb with the strangeness of this whole ceremony thing; this whole *day*. I wonder what happens next? I should have paid more attention on the several occasions when Ruth's tried to talk me through it. . .

Ruth's OK, by the way. Well, I'm pretty certain she's OK. When she arrived at the church with Dad, a few minutes after me and Bethany got here, she told me she was fine. I'm sure it was just a case of the wedding collywobbles. I'm glad she spoke to me about it though, however freaky that was at the time.

"Dearly beloved, we are gathered here today. . ."

God, this is it! The real bit – the real marriage bit! Wow . . . I'm starting to feel a bit sick. . .

Bethany doesn't seem bothered though. She's still singing away softly to herself, waving her wand in time, completely oblivious to the funny man in the white collar and the Big Important Words he's saying.

While I try and get my composure back, I tune in to her little voice.

"*. . .all teachers great and tall. . .!*"

You know, there's nothing like a solemn moment to make the smallest thing unbearably funny. I don't dare look down at Bethany, or I'll just crack up. And I can tell from the way Ruth is trembling gently beside me that the last thing she needs is her rock'n'roll bridesmaid to start sniggering and set off her angel-in-wellies flowergirl.

As the vicar drones on, I try to hold my head high, and concentrate hard on fixing my eyes to something neutral. Unfortunately, my eyes traitorously land on Adam – in his still slightly too big Best Man's suit – who makes everything seventy-zillion times worse by pulling a face and crossing his eyes at me.

As I try to turn my involuntary giggle into a cough, I realize the vicar's suddenly come to the juicy bit – Adam's caught out and is having to scrabble manically in his pocket for the rings, while Ruth turns to me to hand over her bouquet.

Our fingers touch for a second, me and my sister's, and our eyes meet – and in that split-second, I feel a huge hollow emptiness, knowing that the room next door to mine is going to have no one in it now; that I can never just walk in there and ask to borrow her *whatever* again. I won't be able to mosey through, and sit down and chat to her whenever I want. Not that I ever *did* – and now that she's going, I can't understand why I never thought about it. . .

"Repeat after me. . ." says the vicar. "Do you, Ruth –"

And that's it – I'm gone. Tears are spilling unstoppably down my cheeks like a fountain in a thunderstorm.

I can't even stop when I feel an insistent tug at my hand.

"What?" I whisper to Bethany, bending down slightly towards her.

"Why crying, Shaunna?" she whispers back. "Are you hurt?"

"No!" I smile back, though I don't seem to be able to put the brakes on these tears.

I only hope no one else has noticed, only at this rate, I'm going to need sunglasses to hide my red eyes for the photos. . .

"What about Adam's speech?" Dean laughs, doing that sweet, crinkly thing with his nose.

He looks very handsome in his suit, even though I don't normally like suits. Molly looks great too, in a pastel, strappy, chiffony frock that goes amazingly with her white-blonde hair. They look great together – like a dream couple, holding hands easily and smiling at every word the other says.

Nothing like that nice, but awkward, thing me and Dean had. But hey – what a matchmaker I turned out to be, without even trying! If I hadn't dated and dumped him, Molly and Dean might never have happened. It's a real fairy tale – including the fact that I felt like the wicked witch at the time. . .

"Yeah – Adam's speech was . . . something else," I nod, making way as more people arriving for the reception squeeze past me and my voluminous dress.

"God, all that stuff about Wayne getting arrested – that was so funny!" giggles Molly.

It *was* funny – and people *did* laugh like mad at Adam's endless, bad taste jibes throughout his speech about Brian and his underworld connections (ie Wayne). But of course it didn't go down well with everyone. My parents and Mr and Mrs Pindar in particular seemed a little shell-shocked at the prison-related jokes Adam was coming out with, but considering he had five days to think of a speech, I suppose he did pretty well.

Apart from the wisecrack at the end.

Molly must be thinking that very thing right this second.

"Oh, Shaunna – you should have *seen* your face when Adam said—"

Uh-oh. Someone's making some very loud, distorted announcement on the microphone on the small raised stage at the far end of the function room.

"Can everyone gather round, plea-*eeeEEEEEE*!"

Me, Molly and Dean wince (along with everyone else in the room) as eardrum-piercing feedback shrieks through the mike.

"Sorry about that," announces the singer of the band Ruth and Brian have hired. "As I was saying, could everyone gather round, as the bridegroom takes to the floor with his bride. . ."

There's a smattering of applause, but I can hardly hear it for my heart thudding. This is the moment I've been dreading ever since Granny told me about it last week. Not Ruth and Boring Brian doing their wedding waltz; but me and Adam. . .

Oh, God, me and Adam. . .

"It'll be OK! It'll be over in a minute!" Molly tries to reassure me, as she and Dean shepherd me towards the ring of onlookers staring at my sister and her new husband, all alone out there in the middle of the dancefloor.

The band strikes up, into the first bars of a song that no one's going to recognize (from the way the four-piece band are mauling their way through it), but *I* know is The Corrs' *Runaway*, Ruth's favourite record and favourite group in the cosmiverse.

I want to stay in the background, but that's pretty hard, in a vast blue meringue. And whether it's the dress or everyone just somehow knowing it's my turn soon for ritual humiliation, the crowd parts to let me through, for a ringside view of the bride and groom.

They look happy; stupidly happy, gliding and grinning their way round the floor, all doubts on Ruth's side obviously swept away by the fact that the scary part is over and now she's married to the guy she's loved for . . . *for ever*.

I almost feel on the verge of blubbing again, but sheer

terror is stopping me. And speaking of terror, there's Adam, on the other side of the room, getting nudged by his mother, which can only mean one terrible thing. . .

Yep, he's coming over, skirting round the edge of the watching crowd, grinning at me as if this is going to be the best fun next to Space Mountain at DisneyLand.

"Fancy a dance?" he laughs unnervingly in my face.

"No," I hiss, "but I don't have any choice, do I?"

And I let him lead me out on to the dancefloor, where Ruth and Brian stop gazing mushily at each other *just* long enough to give us an encouraging smile. Next thing, I've got one hand held in Adam's, and the other resting uncomfortably on his shoulder.

"Do you know how to do this kind of dancing?" he whispers, like a ventriloquist, through his smile.

"No – I think we'll just have to shuffle from side to side," I suggest softly, my eyes flitting over his shoulder and registering just how many faces were fixed our way. And there were – shoot me now – *loads*.

"Shuffling's all right for *you*," hisses Adam bright and breezily. "Nobody can *see* your feet under that tent. . ."

"Thanks!" I huff, though I'm no big fan of this dress myself. "Oh, and by the way, thanks too for what you said in your speech about me!"

"I said you looked great!" Adam replies, all innocence and arched eyebrows.

"You said I looked *great*," I correct him, "for a person who was dressed in what looked like a cross between a flamenco dancer's frock and a crocheted tea-cosy!"

"Well, come on, Shaunna!" Adam whispers. "You *know* that dress is crap! You'd never willingly choose to wear something like that in a million years, if it hadn't been for your sister!"

That's true, but right now, my loyalty is to Ruth, whatever her taste in clothes and music. Both of which is pretty bad, by the way.

God, when is this rotten song ever going to end and let me escape? I'm sure Andrea Corr never sang as many choruses as this middle-aged, leather-trousered bloke is yodelling his way through.

"This guy's really milking it, isn't he?" says Adam, nodding towards the eyes-closed, mike-clutching crooner, and reading my mind while he's at it.

But I'm not going to respond. Adam's too big-headed and cheeky for his own good, and the sooner I get back to Molly, and hopefully Jude too if she's turned up yet, the better.

"Like this song?" says Adam conversationally, as if he's noticed my silence.

"Like a hole in the head," I mutter back, staring resolutely over his shoulder.

Oh. . .

Oh, God. . .

Suddenly the view over Adam's shoulder is astounding. *Totally* astounding. But as we're shuffling around, that astounding, stupidly wonderful, amazingly unreal view is disappearing. . .

"What're you gawping at?" asks Adam, peering unsubtly around.

"Someone . . . someone I didn't expect to see here," I murmur breathlessly, palpitations tap-dancing their way across my chest.

"Oh, yeah? Like that, is it?" grins Adam, sussing me out straight away. "Someone you fancy?"

"Maybe," I shrug, knowing we're about to shuffle back into a perfect viewing position.

But I can hardly believe it's true – it must have been a figment of my imagination. Why would Star-Boy be at my sister's wedding? But, ahhh . . . there he is again! And he's looking straight over, at me in my blue meringue! And he's . . . he's waving!

"All right!" Adam calls out, letting my hand go just long enough to . . . to wave back at Star-Boy!

"You *know* him?" I blurt out, feeling my legs turn to jelly under my layers of frills and flounce.

"Kevin? Yeah – he's my mate," says Adam matter-of-factly.

Kevin?

I shake my head a little, trying to let this trickle of information sink in. This is the most I've *ever* found out about him. Molly didn't even manage to get this much, after asking around at the party last week; no one she was friendly with knew him or his mates at all.

And now I find Star-Boy is called *Kevin*. . . Surely that can't be right? I don't know what I thought his name would really be, but somehow I never expected Kevin. . .

"Ah, wait a minute!" Adam beams wickedly, realization dawning in that rattling void of a head of his. "You fancy *Kevin*?!"

I stare furiously at Adam, mortified that he's twigged my secret, and desperately trying to think of a convincing denial.

159

"S'pose so. . ." I reply, defeated.

Well, what's the point in pretending? Adam will have been able to tell from the glow-in-the-dark pink flush on my face if nothing else. So, here goes. Here come the sarky comments and the teasing. Humiliation starts here. . .

"I'll introduce you to him, if you like," Adam surprises me by saying, without a hint of teasing in his voice.

I blink at Adam, who's even dropped his dumb Cheshire Cat grin. He really isn't joking; he's genuinely offering to help me out.

Wow. I saw Star-Boy exactly a year ago today, and now I'm *finally* going to meet him.

I take it all back – I'll never call Valentine's Day corny again. . .

chapter seventeen

Long distance love, up close...

Date: *Friday 14th February (later)*

State of mind: *Ecstatic*

Sightings of Star-Boy: *Much, **much** more than just a sighting...*

"...and *he* said hi, and then *I* said hi..."

I'm looking at Molly and Jude, telling them about my first encounter (first of many, I hope) with Star-Boy. OK – *Kevin*.

But as I talk, instead of the faces of my two best mates, all I can see in my mind's eye are those cheekbones close up, that smile, those gorgeous, slightly slanting, dark eyes. Who cares if he doesn't have a beautiful name? He's still the most totally beautiful boy I have ever seen...

"What did he say after that?" asks Jude, who happens to be swaying slightly, I notice.

"Just, 'Catch you later,' 'cause the guys he's with

dragged him off to the bar," I reply.

In a way, I was quite glad that my first introduction to Kevin was so brief; a year's worth of pent-up emotions and expectations were making more than my legs wobble. My voice was so all-over-the-shop I think I'd have sounded like a gerbil on helium if I'd had to say more than just that "hi". At least it gave me a chance to pull myself together. *And* gave me a chance to come and talk it over with the girls, although it had taken ages to find them. But that's weddings for you; having to do the dutiful deed of yakking to endless relatives before you can slip away.

"Shaunna meets Star-Boy. . . I think this calls for a – uck! – celebration drink!" announces Jude, lifting her half-drunk glass of fizzy something-or-other and hiccuping. "I'll just go and get us some more of these. . ."

And off she totters unstably on her high heels. Only she isn't wearing high heels.

"Is she OK?" I ask Molly.

"Absolutely not," says Molly hurriedly. "Scott chucked her again today. Said it was a mistake getting back together."

"Oh. . ." I mutter, watching Jude weave precariously between seats and tables. "Well, *that* reconciliation didn't last too long!"

"I know," nods Molly. "And I *know* it's a good thing in the long run that she's split up from that big dork, but it's hit her really hard."

"Is she *drunk*?" I ask worriedly, now that I've suddenly put two-and-two together and worked out that in Jude's case, being chucked, feeling bad and the availability of free sparkling wine is maybe not such a great combination.

"She's getting that way, I think," Molly pulls a face at me. "Listen; we should both keep an eye on her tonight. Dean will too – and maybe you could ask Adam to watch out for –"

Uh-oh.

So much for pulling myself together. He – Kevin – is headed right towards me and I'm so light-headed it feels as if all the air's been instantly sucked out of my body by aliens on an episode of *The X-Files*.

"Shaunna?" frowns Molly, with her back to my approaching love-god. "What's wrong?"

"It's not wrong; it's right," I squeak, fixing my eyes on her and trying to look casual. (Impossible.)

"What's right?"

"It! It's all right!" I babble, knowing I'm making no sense. "Look, just talk to me – about anything, quickly! Please!"

"*He's* coming over?" Molly widens her eyes, now she understands my babbling code.

"Uh-huh," I mutter.

"So . . . this; this is really pretty!" says Molly, swiftly switching tack and gently lifting the necklace I'm wearing (my bridesmaid's present from Ruth), and studying it closely.

Hurrah for mates who understand what you're going through and just play along. . .

"Hi," says a voice by my side.

"Oh . . . hi!" I say back, hoping that I look suitably surprised. "Um . . . Kevin, this is my friend Molly."

"Hi, Molly," he shrugs in her direction.

"Hi, Kevin," Molly smiles at him, struggling to stop

herself giggling, I can tell.

"You want to dance?"

He's asking me to dance. *Me.* The band are now playing something cheesy that *might* be Whitney Houston's *I Wanna Dance With Somebody*, but whatever it is, from now on it will be my favourite track in the world *ever*.

"Yeah, OK," I nod. "But I'm not promising much. It's kind of hard to dance in a tent."

Kevin grins broadly at me as he walks backwards on to the dancefloor. This is great – I managed to be funny, even if I did hijack Adam's joke to make it happen.

"Well, this band's pretty hard to dance to anyway," says Kevin, leaning in close to my ear to be heard. "They're not going to give U2 much to worry about, are they?"

Great! He's funny too!

But what's *not* funny is this dress. The slow, shuffly waltz with Adam was one thing, but now – when I try and move my hips the way I would dancing normally – the weight of the layers swings the other way, and the petticoats are somehow twisting between my legs. It's as if the top half of my body is working independently from the bottom half and I'm starting to get flustered.

"Sorry – I'm not normally this crap a dancer," I try and joke with Kevin, who's laughing at my attempts to move anything in time to the terrible music. "This dress has got a life of its own. . ."

Kevin's eyes sparkle at me, and I have no idea what to do or say next.

"Well," he smiles, moving towards me, "maybe we'll have to dance like . . . THIS!"

And I'm suddenly breathless again, as Kevin wraps his

arms around my waist, lifts me right off the floor and spins me round madly.

Clutching at his shoulders, all I can make out is a sea of laughing faces . . . apart from one little figure who stands out – Bethany is clapping her hands and jumping up and down in her wellies as she watches her bestest friend fly through the air. . .

"This is better, isn't it?"

You *betcha*.

Me and Kevin, sunk down in a vast, squashy sofa, in a quiet, low-lit, hidden away part of the reception area.

"Yes," I nod in agreement, marvelling at how close we're sitting. "It was getting pretty hot in there. . ."

But I don't think the function room's particularly warm; it's more me that's burning up, with the effort of fooling around and dancing for the last twenty minutes, letting Kevin spin me rock'n'roll style and dip me tango-style and hold me tight salsa-style (very hard in this dress) until we were both laughing so much we had to stop.

"This is pretty comfy, isn't it?" says Kevin, flopping his head back into the mounds of cushions and thudding his feet up on the glass and wood coffee table in front of us.

"Uh-huh," I agree with him, and since I don't know what else to do with them, shove my hands under my bum (again, hard to do in this dress).

"Come on!" Kevin smiles at me, giving me a wicked sideways look. Or maybe it just *looks* wicked because of those almond eyes of his. . .

"Come on what?" I ask him, feeling myself blush apricot pink to match the dress I didn't end up with.

"Get comfy! Put your feet up!" he orders me with a grin.

I smile back, and do as I'm told, resting my blue satin ballet pumps next to his North Face boots. Sticking out under acres of blue dress, white net petticoats and boning, my feet look almost ridiculously small next to them. Or maybe that should be cute... Yes, I hope he thinks they look delicate and cute.

"God, how many layers are there to this thing?" Kevin asks, turning his face to mine and giving me a cheeky look.

"I don't know," I shrug. "I lost count when I was putting it on."

"Shall we count them?" he asks, fixing his eyes on mine.

I don't know what Kevin means, till I feel a pull of material and realize his fingers are slowly gathering up the fabric, exposing lots of hidden away layers as well as my legs.

I giggle nervously and push his hand away, then immediately wish I hadn't. He's only mucking about, and here I am acting like a coy Victorian milkmaid in a Catherine Cookson novel, terrified of the lord's son catching a glimpse of my ankle.

Not that Kevin seems to mind; he's still smiling, and still staring into my eyes.

"Hey," he says softly. "I've got a confession to make..."

"Have you?" I ask, lowering my eyes from his.

Gazing directly into them is like staring straight at the sun. It's too uncomfortable to do, and sets my heart off doing its tap-dancing palpitation routine again.

"Mmm," he mumbles. "I know that you fancy me..."

Uh ... I feel like I just walked through a pair of lift

doors on the twenty-seventh floor and ended up tumbling down the lift shaft. How could he know that? I slap my hands across my face to hide my shame.

"It's OK!" Kevin tries to reassure me. "Adam told me, and I'm glad he did."

Adam. I might have known. That genuine, straightforward-sounding "Do you want me to introduce you?" – of course it wasn't that simple. Of *course* Adam had to go and spoil everything by blabbing the moment my back was turned.

"Hey, Shaunna – it's OK! I'm glad I know!" says Kevin, gently tugging at my wrists.

I give up and let him peel my hands away, but can't bring myself to look at him. But he's not going to allow that either – he cups my face in his hands and . . . and. . .

It's happening. After a year's worth of daydreams and sweet dreams of kissing him, it's finally happening. Every particle in my body goes into meltdown as his lips blend softly into mine, as he moves closer to pull me in towards him. With his chest pushed so close to me, I can feel his heart beating, almost perfectly in synch with mine, and I can smell a mixture of apple shampoo and warm skin, and even the hint of beer adds to the whole, exotic, wondrous mix of it all.

This is tender, this is tingling, this is everything I didn't feel when I kissed Dean. Kevin's lips are like silk and marshmallow and slippery warmth all muddled gloriously together; his hands are strong and sure as they leave my face and slip around my waist, smoothing their way across the slithery material of my dress.

I'm lost in this moment; a moment that's better than

anything I'd ever imagined in this long, longing-filled year. I don't ever want it to end, but I know it will, and that doesn't matter because I'll have the luxury of this memory now; I can replay it in my mind over and over and over—

Snappppppp!

And that's the end of *that* lovely thought.

"Kevin!" I yelp, trying to extricate his hand from down the front of my plunging sweetheart neckline. "Stop! What are you doing?! *Stop* it!"

Good grief, I *am* the corseted heroine of a Catherine Cookson novel, trying desperately to stop myself being ravished by the lord's heartless cad of a son. Only those storylines always seemed a bit of a joke, and this definitely doesn't.

"Kevin!" I yelp again, pushing at him with all my strength, but he's half on top of me, kissing at my neck while he's wrestling his way into my dress and pretending he's gone deaf.

"Leave me ALONE!" I gasp, using every ounce of energy and throwing him back on to his side of the sofa.

"Jesus!" Kevin sneers at me. "What's that all about?!"

"Me making a big mistake," I say shakily, jumping to my feet and jerkily smoothing my ruffled dress down.

"Tell me about it," he laughs, with a blunt, hard edge to his voice.

I'm just about to hurry away when I see the glint of something on the floor. It's too close to him – it'd be like reaching inside a lion's cage. But I have to get it back; that necklace was a present from someone who cares about me, which Kevin certainly doesn't. He didn't even care that he'd snapped the chain as he'd tried to fumble his way down my top.

Moving faster than I thought would be possible in such a boned bundle of material, I swoop down, grab my broken gift and run away, padding back to the safety of the function room as fast as my blue ballet pumps will carry me. . .

For the past half-hour, I've been stuck talking to Granny, her friend Marjorie (me and Adam weren't the only ones allowed to invite friends – although I wish Adam hadn't bothered), my uncle Eric and Auntie Barbara. I'd rather have been with Molly or Jude, but I couldn't find them – or Dean – when I came scurrying back into the room after my tussle with Kevin.

Still, chit-chatting about how lovely the day's been and how pretty the garlands of doves strung everywhere are, and how gorgeous Ruth looks; it's given me a chance to calm down and stop hyperventilating. But even so, the way I'm feeling at the moment, I don't know how I can ever get over what just happened. Not so much the fact that Kevin turned into Lech of the Century – although that was pretty upsetting – it's more that I can't believe I got it so *wrong*. How did the Star-Boy I yearned over all this time turn into creepy, sleazy Kevin? I feel like such a total fool. . .

"Shaunna – have you seen Jude?" Molly hisses suddenly in my ear, while still managing to smile brightly at Granny.

"No. But I'm *so* glad to see *you*," I tell her, getting up from my seat, and then remembering my manners and excusing myself. "Sorry, Granny, sorry everyone – I've just got to go and talk to Molly about something."

I've just slipped my arm into Molly's and started walking away when our way is blocked, by none other than Adam – who I'd rather not talk to right now, since him going and opening his mouth practically gave Kevin the green light to *molest* me.

"Shaunna – it's Jude!" Adam blurts out.

Instantly, I forget to be angry with him – by the look on his face something is really wrong.

"What's happened?" asks Molly. "I've been looking everywhere for her!"

"My mate Stephen," says Adam agitatedly, "he says she's in a right mess, *really* hammered."

"Drunk, you mean?" I check.

"As a skunk," he nods.

"That's what was worrying me!" says Molly. "Last time I saw her she was slow-dancing out in the hallway with . . . with. . ."

She shoots me a look, and it's obvious that she's hesitating about using a certain person's name. But I can guess who.

"Kevin?" I help her out.

She nods slowly, trying to work out from my face how I feel about that piece of news.

"It's OK. . ." I shrug, knowing I can hardly fill her in on everything that happened to me right at this second. "So why were you worried?"

"Well," Molly continues, "she just seemed so wasted, and they were slow dancing, even though you couldn't hear the band properly out there. He – Kevin – just seemed to be propping her up more than anything. I had to go to the loo, and was going to try and sort her out when I came out, but she – they – had disappeared. . ."

"Listen!" Adam interrupts urgently. "I know where they are! Kevin was boasting to Stephen that he was going to take Jude to a hotel bedroom, the one Brian and Ruth are using!"

The one they hired to get changed in later on, I realize, before they leave for their honeymoon. . .

"But it'll be locked; how can Kevin get in there?" I ask in a panic, remembering my own wrestling match with Kevin, and thinking about how drunk and vulnerable Jude must be right now. "He'd need a key, wouldn't he?"

"He's got one," sighs Adam, slapping his hand on his forehead. "I got him to help me earlier, when I snuck in there to put confetti in their suitcases and everything. He locked up, and said he'd hand the key back to reception, but I guess he hasn't."

"Come on then; we'd better hurry. . ." I mutter, lifting my skirts and rushing ahead of the other two, and hoping we aren't too late. . .

I'm getting to be a good actress; when I asked Ruth if I could borrow the key to her room, I didn't alarm her and tell her it was because we were trying to rescue Jude before the lethal combination of alcohol and Kevin got her into more trouble than she knew how to handle.

Oh, no; I told her the excitement of the day had given me a headache, and I needed to get away and lie down for ten minutes, till the Nurofen I'd taken worked. She just smiled and said fine, passing me the key out of her little pearl handbag and not questioning why Molly and Adam seemed to be coming with me.

"Here – let me do it!" says Adam, when my trembling hand can't get the key into the lock.

Gratefully, I stand back and let him help, my heart thundering so loud I can't understand why no one else seems to hear it.

"What the f—"

Kevin leaps off the bed – and off Jude – as soon as we all pile in the door. Luckily, Jude doesn't seem to have any clothes where they shouldn't be, ie we seem to have arrived before any attempts on Kevin's part to peel them off her.

"Shaunna? Mol?" Jude mumbles woozily, as if she's not entirely sure where she is or what's happening.

As me and Molly rush to her side, I hear a voice, quavering in rage, yell, "You! Outside! *Now!*"

How strange to hear Adam – the goofy guy, the joker – turn so white-hot with anger. . .

chapter eighteen

*Love, doves and
funny Valentines...*

Date:	*Friday 14th February (much later)*
State of mind:	*Battered and bruised*
Sightings of Star-Boy:	*Urgh, please no...*

"We're lucky, you and me," Molly whispers, as we stand in the corridor, just outside the hotel bedroom.

Inside, curled up and dozing on the bed is Jude, freshly showered, all wrapped up in a fluffy hotel dressing gown, with the coffee we made her drink swilling around her bloodstream while she sleeps off the worst of the alcohol. We're going to take shifts to watch over her, me and Mol – give her an hour or two till the party winds down, and by that time she should be well enough to bundle into a cab with us and go home.

"Why are we lucky?" I whisper back, my dress rustling loudly as I cross my arms.

173

"We've got ordinary parents," Molly shrugs. "Not very exciting parents, but at least they're vaguely interested in us. And they'll sometimes even listen if we want to talk or moan. Poor Jude doesn't have that."

It's true. Jude's got a dad she never sees and a mum who's so groovy she's too busy having fun to pay any attention to her daughter, and how she might be getting on. Or *not* getting on, as the case may be.

"Do you think that's part of the reason she's in such a mess tonight?" I frown, trying to figure out what Molly's getting at.

"No – but I think it's why she's got zero confidence in herself, and was so grateful to Scott for going out with her."

"And now so devastated that he's finished with her," I finish Molly's train of thought. "Do you think that's why she ended up with Kevin tonight? Trying to boost her self-esteem after getting dumped?"

"Makes sense, doesn't it?" Molly raises her blonde eyebrows at me. "Course the booze didn't help. I don't think she even realized *who* she was with, Shaunna."

"Guess not," I nod, knowing that Jude would never have gone after my Star-Boy if her brain hadn't been swimming in cheap champagne. Not that I wanted him any more – but she wasn't to know that.

Poor Jude. Me and Molly will have to take *extra* good care of her after this; try and get her to see that she's worth *ten* Scott Masons and *twenty* Kevins, and that even if her mum and dad have failed their parenting exams, it doesn't mean that *she's* in any way a failure.

And when she sobers up and cringes at the close call

she had with Kevin, the first thing I'm going to do is tell her *I* was there too – only I was a whole lot stupider, wasting an entire year drooling over someone who wasn't worth *talking* to, never mind lusting after.

But then the really sad, pathetic thing is, the Star-Boy I was crazy about didn't even exist – I just made him up in my head after a few snatched sightings of a boy who turned out to be a beautiful, repulsive *moron*. . .

"Anyway, come back in twenty minutes," says Molly, checking her watch. "We'll see how she's doing then."

"OK," I nod, impulsively giving Molly a quick hug.

Hey, in every way possible, it's been an emotional day. . .

"How's things?" I say, hoisting up my skirts and joining Adam on the cold, granite step out in the dark garden, where four hours ago we were saying "cheese" and freezing, while the wedding photographer snapped his reams of film.

"Oh, pretty crap," shrugs Adam, staring off into the distance.

I'd been on my way back to the function room a few seconds ago, when I spotted him through the French windows, sitting bathed in the yellowy lights that dotted the darkness of the garden and slouched under the weight of sheer misery.

"That bad, huh?" I say lightly, trying to make him smile. It doesn't work. "So, what happened to Kevin?"

"He's long gone," Adam mumbles flatly. "That's *it* with him and me."

I'm not sorry to hear that. But I wouldn't be so tactless

175

as to say that out loud. Whatever I think of Kevin, him and Adam are mates. Or *were* mates, I should say. . .

"How long have you known him, then?" I ask, avoiding using Kevin's actual name in case it makes me gag.

"Years. It's just that crowd thing, isn't it?" says Adam, sounding sad and empty. "You hang out together, but then you just start to outgrow some people. It's been like that for a while now with me and Kev. The last year really, I guess he's just been hacking me off more and more. And tonight, pulling that stunt with Jude – and then he goes and tries to make an excuse for himself by telling me that he only went after her 'cause *you* knocked him back!"

I start shivering, partly because it's February and freezing out here, but mostly because the very memory of loving Star-Boy and being groped by Kevin is making me feel pretty sick. . .

"You told him I fancied him," I confront Adam – but quietly, not accusingly. "He said so."

"I told him you *liked* him," Adam says irritably, but I can tell it's not me he's irritated with. "Jeez – what's Kev like? He's got such a *weird* attitude towards women; he's always boasting about how far he gets with girls, as if we're all supposed to be *impressed* or something."

Lucky escape, lucky escape, lucky escape. . . I intone silently in my head.

"You know one thing he did?" Adam laughs, without a trace of humour in his voice. "The one thing that made me think, nah – me and you are going in different directions, mate?"

"What was that?" I ask, huddling myself up to conserve heat. I'm tempted to pull the top layer of my dress up and wrap it around my shoulders like a shawl to keep me warm.

"About a year ago – must have been . . . oh, maybe around January or February," Adam elaborates, still staring off in to the gardens, "me and my mates, we used to sneak into Westburn Park at nights, just for somewhere to hang out."

Instantly – as soon as Adam says that – loads of images start flicking through my head, like a slide show. Star-Boy and his mates at the party last week – that was Kevin and his cronies (minus Adam, who was out at the disastrous stag party). Star-Boy passing me that day in the department store, when I was getting my '80s makeover – it was Kevin, with some of the other lads I've seen here tonight. Star-Boy at the festival in Westburn Park – it wasn't a coincidence that Adam was so close by, ready to pick me up; he'd been there with Kevin, as well as the drunk lads who'd floored me. Star-Boy passing me that day in the café nearly a year ago, when I was still wearing the floral circlet on my head after the wedding fayre – Kevin was with that lad here tonight called Stephen. And Star-Boy star-gazing in the park last Valentine's Day – what was the story behind that? I'm trembling with cold and anticipation, knowing I'm about to find out. . .

"Go on," I say encouragingly. "You were all hanging out in Westburn Park. . ."

"Yeah, well, Kevin had found this old telescope in a box in his garage. And you know what he used it for?"

"No," I mumble.

Whatever Kevin was staring at, it wasn't the rings of Saturn, or the swirling red dust of Mars, or the deep, unfathomable recesses of the moon like I'd imagined. *That* much I think I can guess, now. . .

"You know that tower-block on the far side of the park?" Adam turns and looks at me finally.

I nod. I know it.

"He used to spy on this woman on the eighth floor, who wandered round her flat in the nude with the curtains open. She probably thought no one could see her, but there was Kevin, night after night, ogling at her through his telescope."

What was it Jude had said that night about Star-Boy? That he looked dodgy; that he might be one of the park perverts her neighbours were always so worried about. She was right. In fact, all her nosy old neighbours were right. *I* was the one who was wrong, staring long-distance at Star-Boy through rose-tinted specs about a metre thick. And I thought it was *Jude* who had no common-sense when it came to boys.

God, I'm so *dumb*. . .

"Hey, are you OK?" asks Adam, coming out from under his cloud of gloom now that he's seen one settle over me.

"Kind of," I shrug, knowing I can never tell him what a fool I am. "It's been a funny old day. . ."

"Tell you what *was* funny," I hear Adam say.

"What?" I ask, shivering and staring my red-face down at the ground.

"You and me."

"Huh?"

I spin round towards him, without thinking.

"Well," he begins, breaking into one of his ear-to-ear grins, "*you* stomping around in that blue parachute and *me* – I look like a kid dressing up in his dad's suit in this thing!"

It *is* funny. The suit jacket's made for rugby-playing, beer-belly proportioned Wayne – not skinny, tall Adam.

"Yeah, we wouldn't win the Elle Style Awards, would we?" I find myself smiling back at him.

"And us trying to waltz! It's a wonder we didn't get arrested for fraud – two elephants on rollerblades would make a better job of waltzing than us!"

"*Tell* me about it," I laugh.

There's silence for a second, as we sit companionably shivering together.

"Cold?" asks Adam, reading my mind.

"A bit," I admit, although I'm in no hurry to get back inside to the merriment, after the weirdness of what's happened in the last while.

"C'mere," says Adam, suddenly standing, and taking a few steps on to the crunchy, frost-tipped lawn.

"What?" I ask, although I'm already up and following him.

"Let's give it another go, now no one's staring at us!" he grins, pulling me into the looky-likey waltz position we'd struggled with earlier.

"No!" I try to protest, coming over all shy, even though there's only a couple of ornamental stone lions watching us.

"Wait!" he says, not letting me go. "I've figured out how to do this, without us standing on each other's feet!"

"OK, how?!" I demand.

"Well, first you've got to stand on my feet!"

"What are you on about?!"

"Go on – stand on my feet, and I'll waltz round with you!"

And so I do. I haven't done this since I was little, fooling around to something or other on the radio with my dad.

"You'll regret this!" I giggle, stepping my ballet pumps on to his black suede shoes. "The dress probably weighs more than I do!"

"*Uhhhh. . .*" Adam groans, pretending to crumple under the combined tonnage of me and the meringue.

And then he straightens up, hauling one foot up and then the other, with me balanced on top, and moves round in a slow, ungainly circle, not helped by the fact that I'm giggling so much that we might over-balance.

"Enough!" I laugh, slipping my feet back on to the frost-covered grass, but somehow, we keep dancing.

"Where's that thing you were wearing?" Adam suddenly asks, staring down at my chest.

"My necklace?" I answer, surprised that he'd even noticed it. "I gave it to my granny to look after. The chain snapped."

I hope he doesn't ask *how* the chain snapped.

"Shame; it was pretty. What was it – some kind of bird?" he surprises me again with his observational skills.

"A dove," I tell him. "Made out of snow quartz."

At least that's what it said inside the box. A tiny snow-white dove carved out of snow quartz. Who'd have thought Ruth would give me something so lovely? And who knew I'd learn to love doves?

I'm feeling strangely shy again, as another silence settles over us.

"I was pretty surprised at the way you yelled at . . .

Kevin," I finally say.

"Were you?" asks Adam, blinking grey-blue eyes at me. "How come?"

"I guess I'm just not used to seeing you serious," I shrug, as we continue our music-less, slow spinning. "You're usually always . . . goofing around."

"Am I?" Adam grins, as if I've paid him a huge compliment. "Well, coming from a family like mine, it's kind of *tempting* to goof around."

"What do you mean?"

"Don't get me wrong – I love my parents and my brother and sister," he says hurriedly, "but they can be pretty . . . *boring*. That's when I get the urge to shake things up a bit; try and get everyone laughing. But they usually just end up getting annoyed with me."

Wow – that could almost be *me* talking.

"Sometimes, I think the only one I've got anything in common with is Bethany," he continues. "I mean, I know she can be a pain in the ass, but at least she's fun to hang out with. Until my sister tells me to stop winding her up, of course."

I smile to myself, thinking of the times I've seen Adam chasing Bethany around, acting like a big kid and having a better time than all the adults put together.

"Speaking of Lynsey; you know she wants to kill you, don't you?" Adam suddenly announces.

"The wellies?" I grin, realizing I've finally been found out.

"Uh-huh," Adam nods soberly. "You are *not* the number one favourite person with my family over that one. Expect when it comes to Bethany, of course. And me."

That "And me" . . . he didn't mean anything by it, but it's unnerved me all the same. I have to say something fast, before I start blushing again.

"Speaking of your family," I start, "I'm glad the thing with Molly and Dean worked out."

"Not as glad as I am," Adam laughs, and then stops.

Stops dancing too.

"Meaning?" I squeak softly.

"Meaning, I hated seeing you and him together," Adam blinks rapidly at me. "Almost as much as I hated it when you said you fancied Kevin."

"Oh. . ." I say, though it comes out more like a little surprised sigh.

Adam says nothing, just blinks some more at me. I can feel how fast he's breathing, and I don't know what to do.

Or maybe I do.

Maybe, just maybe what I should do is move towards him like *this*, and then tilt my head ever so slightly, just to see what it feels like to kiss someone who's funny, and sweet and special. . .

And it feels nice. Warm and soft and nice. Maybe my molecules haven't melted, but then I don't know if that's entirely safe anyway. No – I think I like this better . . . kissing Adam is gentle and tender and totally wonderful.

"Shaunna! Shaunna! Is that you out there!"

Mum's voice cuts through the moment and we leap apart, startled and shocked, but grinning madly at each other.

"Yes, Mum!" I call back, as me and Adam pad towards the French doors of the hotel.

"Oh, you're there too, are you, Adam?" says my mum,

putting her hands on her hips. "Well, I've got a bone to pick with both of you. . ."

Me and Adam swap frowns. What is it? Is it the wellie situation? Or the fact that Jude is snoring off a hangover in the bridal suite?

"*We* have just been watching the wedding video," Mum says sternly. "And would you mind telling me what you two were doing pulling faces and giggling in the middle of the vows?"

Adam looks worriedly at me, and then slowly crosses his eyes.

Mum tuts loudly and rolls her eyes as we both crack up, stomping back off to the reception as we follow doubled up behind her.

Just in front of the doors to the reception, Adam and I get our breath back and try to compose ourselves, ready for whatever we're about to face.

"Fancy making an entrance?" grins Adam, squeezing my hand.

"Absolutely!" I reply, not a clue what he's on about but more than happy to go along with him.

"Step on board, then!" he orders me, pointing to his shoes.

And with that we crash through the doors, Adam stomping out a vague approximation of a waltz while I stand on his toes and hang on for dear life. . .

My grumpy Granny McKay; when she's not too busy cleaning anything that doesn't move, going in and out of mourning and reeling off lists of botanical names, she likes to do the typical granny thing and trot out sayings in that knowledgeable, it's-all-true-you-know! grandmother-type way. One of her favourites is "Good things come to those who wait", and you know something? I think I like that one.

After all, it maybe took me a year, but I ended up with something – sorry, someone – pretty good, pretty special. And maybe it wasn't Star-Boy, but I have ended up with Adam, my very own funny Valentine. . .

about the author

In her teens, Karen McCombie vowed three things: one, to be an artist; two, never to move away from Scotland; and three, never to get married. Strangely enough, she is now a full-time author living in leafy north London with her husband, Tom.

The lure of work on magazines such as J17 and Sugar was the reason for the move south, and after several years in journalism, Karen turned her attention to fiction, writing the best-selling series Ally's World, as well as Stella Etc. and many more teen titles.

In her spare time, Karen likes to stop and pat cats in the street, even though she has three at home.